Smashing Laptops

(a Nomad's Romance with Missoula)

Impossible Clock Productions

other works by the author

fiction

THE ADVENTURES OF THE IMAGINATION
OF PERIPHERY STOWE

DEADWIND SEA

plays

SALEP & SILK

comics and graphic novels

FICTION CLEMENS

WALLED IN

SKY PIRATES OF NEO TERRA

24SEVEN, VOL. 2
(CONTRIBUTING WRITER)

OUTLAW TERRITORY, VOL. 1 & 2
(CONTRIBUTING WRITER)

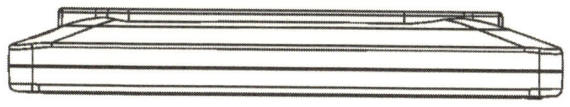

Smashing Laptops

a Nomad's Romance with Missoula

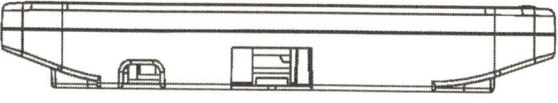

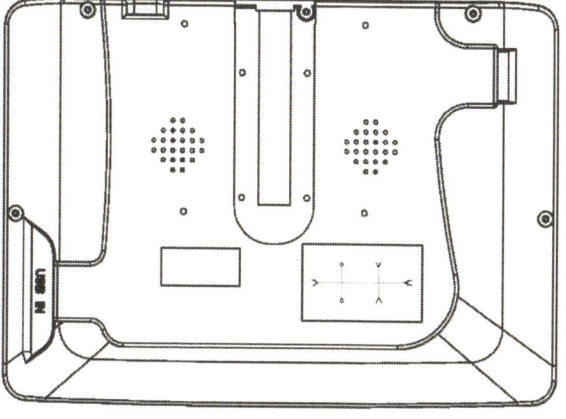

by

Josh
Wagner

Chapter Two, Section 0: *Santa Cruz* first appeared as
"Salt of the Earth" in CAFE IRREAL vol. 10, 2003

Chapter Four, Section 5 first appeared as
"Smashing Laptops" the short story in CEDILLA vol. 2, 2008

"Raiding the Ritz" was originally published in SLUMGULLION vol. 3, 2007

"SMASHING LAPTOPS" is a work of fiction except for the parts that aren't.

Impossible Clock Productions, LLC.
Somewhere in Montana
www.joshwagner.org
Cover Photography © 2011 by Marshall Hibbard
Cover Design by Marshall Hibbard
Zozezaz Diagram by Anthony Gregori
Title Page Design by Tim Daniel
"Growing Song" © 2011 by Katie Ludwick (ladypajama)
Illustration "Layered Universe" © 2011 Katie Ludwick (ladypajama)
Illustration "Quit Looking Drunk" © 2011 Katie Ludwick (ladypajama)
Illustration "Hello Alien" © 2011 Katie Ludwick (ladypajama)
Illustration "Snail Shroom" © 2011 Josh Ludwick
Photos from the "Blasting Typewriters" series © 2011 Josh Wagner
Photo "Pickaxe and Telephone Wires" © 2011 Rebecca Schaffer
Illustration "Windmill" © 2011 Tommy Galyean
Photo on final page, "Lucyfurr Finds Brains" © 2011 Brad Wilson

Publisher's Cataloging-in Publication Data
Wagner, Josh
    SMASHING LAPTOPS (A NOMAD'S ROMANCE WITH MISSOULA) / Josh
Wagner -- Missoula, MT : Impossible Clock Productions, 2011
    ISBN: 978-1463712631
    1. Literature. 2. Memoir. 3. Schwoogle.

Dedicated to Jesus Danger Christ Ludwick-Jennings

Acknowledgements

I sat down and tried to write out a list of all the people without whom this book would not exist. There are far too many of you. I can't possibly name you all. I hope you know who you are.

I must, however, heap worlds of gratitude upon Sarah Jennings, Claire Mikeson, Joshua Hamilton, Brian Buckbee and Coleman Pape for providing close readings and spectacular advice on early drafts.

Thank you, Missoula. I'll miss you when I go.

"They have pretty blue flowers over there.
Swarms of little, pretty blue flowers...
I guess they blame those on the Russians, too."

- Lisle Mueller Chestnutt (1916 – 2010)

"And if I die in Raleigh at least I will die free."

- Old Crow Medicine Show

PROLOGUE

Once when I lived in San Francisco I came across a group of street kids who slept on the Haight. They stretched out along the side of a building, seven of them in a line sharing one cigarette. They had a dog, but the dog didn't smoke. I sat down next to them and got into a heated discussion about Batman. They explained that they were vigilantes, and it was their job to keep the Haight straight. "Dudes piss on people's doors or mess with girls—we put a stop to it."

None of these kids were a day over 18, so I smiled and listened but didn't think much of it until a little while later this pair of dreaded-out hippies walked by. As they crossed the street, one of them tossed a beer bottle, shattering it on the concrete. Well, these street kids were up like lightning and a second later they formed a tight little circle around the hippies. I thought there'd be a fight, but instead one of the vigilantes, all broad shouldered in spiked leather, explained to the hippies in a rational tone of voice exactly why breaking bottles on the street was bad for everybody. He said, "Not only is it stupid, but that kind of shit brings the cops. Then they start harassing everyone more and more, and the Haight turns into a bad place to be."

Earlier that week I'd passed two officers talking to an old man snuggled up in a doorway with his sleeping bag.

As I walked by I heard one of the cops say, "You need to put the pipe away or we'll have to take it." That's how chill this place was. And the street kid was right. Start breaking beer bottles for no good reason and all of that changes.

Anyway, the whole scene ended up with the hippies saying they understood and they were sorry. They cleaned up the broken glass and everyone, vigilantes and hippies alike, engaged in a round of hugs.

It was the most beautiful thing I've ever seen, and I fell in love with San Francisco.

There is no moment like this by which I define the little city of Missoula, Montana. She is too close. Missoula is not the lover you meet in the rain for a torrid night of passion and never see again. Missoula is the blanket you wrap yourself up in every night until you've nearly forgotten she exists. It's only when you find yourself in bed without her that you realize just how important she was every day of your life.

I remember climbing up to the "M" after a three-day fast, taking mushrooms and looking down on Missoula as if she were a toy city beneath a Christmas tree.

I remember Jays Upstairs, where you could go to a rock show and do your laundry at the same time.

I remember wandering through town under a quiet snowfall after all the power had gone out.

I remember the homeless Salish man who carved me a cane on the walking bridge. And the white-eyed Indian who changed my entire night and possibly my entire life by saying, "Don't be afraid," as he walked past me near the river.

I remember getting lost in Missoula long after I thought I'd walked every street and seen every corner. To lose my bearings in a place so familiar felt no less disorienting than if I had stumbled around the bend to find a midnight Pakistani bazaar selling shrunken heads and dried centipedes. Even in a small town there are enough nooks to last the rest of your life, though you may require a magnifying glass to find them.

I remember Missoula's very own Leprechaun offering business card wishes from behind his beard.

I remember bowling with wine bottles on the Northside.

I remember the night Levi brought my dog Lucyfurr to me days after I'd decided I wasn't responsible enough to keep her. He said, "The guy who adopted her is a dick, so I kidnapped her and now she's yours." And she was my traveling companion for 8 years.

I remember chasing girls and making up stories. I remember two drunk kids who took us out to the woods and gave a sermon on Bill Burroughs and Louisiana and spewed whisky on the fire and seasoned our acid with charisma until the sky paled blue and we returned haggard and pathetic to Finnegan's.

I remember the great bee massacree of '93.

I remember book battles at the Colonel Fun Show, wine-drunk, where me and Dean mashed up sex manuals with cookbooks, and Pynchon with Seuss.

I remember offering french fries to strangers with Bosco, and trading random shit from the drawer for a rubber chicken and a bucket of beer.

I remember falling in love night after night after night. You women are all so beautiful it makes a guy wonder what he's even doing on this planet.

I have enough memories of Missoula to bore you a thousand times over, but there is no defining moment. Believe me, I'd tell you if there was.

CHAPTER ONE

KATIE LUDWICK

1.

"HEADING home?" the girl at the ticket office asked me.

"Yeah, I forgot my jacket," I said. I had been trying to be funny, but I was actually kind of serious so the joke didn't work. She just stared at me like I was crazy.

It's early September, 2:17am. Forty-eight miles outside Missoula, Montana. My greyhound departed from that Las Vegas ticket office what seems like a hundred hours ago. Now we've stopped in the dark shadows of pine trees. Yellow light winces through the fog. My forehead stamped against the cold glass.

I'm totally broke. I've never been so broke in my life. No dollar bills crumpled up in pockets, no quarters floating around my backpack. Not even a blank check to bounce. I try to cram my legs into a comfortable position in the impossibly awkward greyhound seat. No one gets off, no one gets on. Lights out. I stare through the dirty window at haggard shapes watching from wood porches and chairs that have sat around for decades. I close my eyes and wait for the bus to start moving again.

I'm going home. Back to Montana. Back where it's safe and quiet. Back where I belong.

I'm kidding myself. I don't belong here. But then, neither does anyone else.

Only bears and wildflowers belong in Montana.

2.

It took me almost six weeks to escape Vegas. Probably the longest six weeks of my life. It was 112 degrees and not even August the day I finally decided to make my way back to Missoula. I'd been sitting in a small studio apartment on Tropicana all afternoon, slumped in front of five fans and a swamp cooler. Together they worked it like a junkyard band. My thoughts tripped through the obstacle of their rhythm. I swore my eternal devotion to Montana's crabby climate, envisioned her lush arteries, and occasionally spritzed my face with a green plastic squirt gun.

Spending a summer in Las Vegas is not something one decides to do. It's something that happens quick and brutal like a mugging—when your eye is on a woman's ass, your head is in the clouds, and your legs are marching lockstep to the four-letter heartbeat of the single cause and cure for all of mankind's ills. I'd fallen in love. That's another thing I don't recommend trying out in Vegas. When it doesn't work out the game feels rigged, like the sting of house odds. Thanks for playing. Come back when you've got more to lose! Loss is a religion in Vegas, I don't care if it's money, sanity, or a woman.

I could think of nothing better to do in that lonely Las Vegas meltdown than lock myself away from the sun and think about rolling stones and how much harder it was each day to get out of my chair. This wasn't me. This was the lump that love left over. I needed to move, but nothing moved me.

Correction: I no longer believe there's any such thing as "losing" a woman. A man loses himself as women slip into the future.

Spread out among piles of empty boxes, I was wondering for the millionth time how it had all come down to this when the phone rang.

I found it under a pile of dirty towels and lifted it off its cradle. I could hear Katie Ludwick, my old friend from back in Montana, breathing on the other end of the line. She did not say hello. Or rather, she did say hello, but she said it like this: "I'm pregnant."

3.

The Katie Ludwick in my mind is six inches taller than the Katie Ludwick of flesh and blood. She wears an iron girdle, and a buckler dangles alongside a fiery orange skirt sewn from sundry reptilian skins. Her valkyrie white hair cracks like a willow branches in the wind. Storm clouds and flash mobs reflect in her eyes. She breaks walnut shells with her teeth and then spits them out because she hates walnuts. She is always standing on the edge of some cliff.

Photos reveal a different story. In this one her eyes are calm, delighted. Here she patiently tinkers with a sewing machine. Cross-legged on the floor she reads the Outlaw Bible of American Poetry or clips photos from National Geographic. She is five foot five inches tall, with shoulder length dishwater blonde hair, wide hips and a moderate portion of flab that hangs over the lip of her pants. She has a snaggletooth and chapped lips. Freckles. Her eyes are muddy green. After a good cry her cheeks puff up like pomegranates. She likes walnuts but can't eat them because she is allergic.

I've known Katie Ludwick most of my life. She's my best friend's little sister and that sort of makes her my little sister too.

That afternoon on the phone Katie laughed like a

little lunatic and I could hear her scratching her briar patch hair into an even bigger briar patch. "I can't have babies, Josh! I'll make a terrible mother. I don't like to take care of people. I'm not a caring person. I'm not compassionate. I'm selfish. I always want things to go my way."

I could relate.

"Come home," she said.

"I will," I said.

"For reals?"

"I'm broke," I said.

"I'm broken," she said.

"Pregnant is not broken."

"Something feels broken."

"It's like the opposite of broken," I said.

"Just come home."

"I'll find a way."

"Promise?"

"I'll find a way."

In her entire life Katie Ludwick has only had one boyfriend. His name is Adam Jostler. They've been living together for a while now, and he is not the father of her child.

Before hanging up the phone, Katie told me how she found out about her condition. She'd only gone to see her doctor on account of stomach problems and lethargy. Plagued by a dozen food allergies, Katie worried over what she would have to give up this time. The doctor told her to sit down. A nurse brought her some water.

The doctor diagnosed no new allergy. Instead she found the tides of nature tumbling, all inward instruments tuning, turning to the twist of hidden clocks.

When the doctor told her she was pregnant, all Katie could say was, "Oh."

Stumbling out of the waiting room, she bumped into a table, spilling a jigsaw puzzle onto the floor.

Once she was back among friends, she quietly endured their coos and congratulations. She dodged questions about the father's identity. Not out of embarrassment, but out of confusion. The father of Katie's new fetus had no identity. But this wasn't a case of too many possible lovers to choose from. There were too few.

Our little Katie was a virgin.

4.

The nouveau lights come on and the air-brakes fizzle, waking me up. The hulking mass of bus driver's silhouette looms incandescent.

"Greyhound: We don't give a fuck because you don't give a fuck."

"What?" The question squeezes through my half-glued eyelids.

"I said everyone has to get off here, sir," the driver parrots with all the enthusiasm of a broken toothpick. "Take your bags, valuables, and belongings with you. Greyhound is not responsible for the loss or theft of any bags, valuables, or belongings."

"Where are we?"

He doesn't answer. He's already down the aisle rustling up the next passenger.

Every place looks the same through a Greyhound window. I only know I'm in Missoula because I just know.

Besides Katie there's another reason I'm going home, and that's to get my jacket. It's one of those 80s faded blue denims with a comfy grey lining. Torn to tatters, covered in safety pins. A thick grey hood and broken cinch strings. I call it a boxer's jacket because my best friend Dean wore it in high school and back then he was a boxer. But maybe it's just that connection making me think it looks like a boxer's jacket. Maybe it doesn't look like a boxer's jacket at all. As far as I know there isn't any such thing as a boxer's jacket.

I left the jacket in Montana because Katie said she'd take care of it while I was gone. I can only hope she's too pregnant to wear it or I might not get it back at all. Me and Katie Ludwick, we're both in love with the same jacket.

God, I miss that jacket. I think things in Vegas would have gone better if I'd had it with me. I sometimes wonder if my subconscious schemed for all that drama to go down just so I'd have a good excuse to come home. Of course, Katie Ludwick's belly is the main reason for my trip. She's been carrying that fatherless child for eight months now, and I swore an oath I'd be there when she delivers.

All I know now is I need to see Katie Ludwick and I need to get that jacket. That's why you turn around and go back, to get the things you left behind.

5.

From Seattle another bus is scheduled to arrive. On that bus is a girl I've known almost as long as I've known Katie Ludwick. Amelia is who I tell my secrets to. Well, most of them anyway. We're like twins from mirror universes. Exactly alike in opposite ways. She worked it all out so we would arrive at the same time: me from the south and her from the west. This was the plan she insisted on when she called me: We'll meet in Missoula on separate greyhounds, she said. Let's not tell anyone we're coming back, she said. No one to meet us at the station but each other. We'll both pretend we've come to pick the other up. It'll be a riot, she said.

When Amelia hugs me and says, *welcome back to Missoula*, and I say, *how was your trip*, she'll respond with something like, *it hasn't been the same around here since you've been gone*, and I'll give her a comforting, *I'll bet you're tired, I've got the couch all set up for you*.

My bus was supposed to roll in at ten, but Idaho Falls turned out to be a "breakdown stop". Greyhound has pickup stops, meal stops, and breakdown stops.

I couldn't call Amelia from the road to tell her I'd be late because I don't have a cell phone and we've reached the technological cusp where I no longer understand pay phones. Logically I understand them. You put quarters in and the phone decides how long you get to talk. But emotionally I've lost touch. I can no longer bring myself to use one.

"Oh My God, we broke down too!" Amelia couldn't be happier. She'd only been waiting on me for about a half hour. "This invasion was planned by providence."

Amelia's hair is a bright burgundy, freshly dyed. Wild, lilting eyes perch upon high cheekbones like statues edging a forest grove. They stand as tall as human eyes can possibly stand. An haute couture jacket way beyond her pay grade buckles over a goodwill T-shirt and plaid skirt. Black boots to her knees—the heels of a bull.

I say, "You really didn't tell anyone you were coming?"

"That was our plan. Did you tell anyone?" Amelia's voice is soft, stern, and precise. Like a fourth grade teacher.

"Nope."

"Good. Let's call someone. I'm not carrying this big-ass bag all the way down Broadway."

Her bag was indeed big-ass. Army duffle bag, packed to the gills. What is it with girls?

"What is it with girls?" I say. "I thought you were only staying a few days."

"I have...things," she says, polishing her hands over the bag's canvas surface as if the gesture explained it all.

"Wasn't our plan to walk into town all anonymous like?"

"Yeah. Let's not." From her Hello Kitty purse Amelia produces a pack of American Spirits. She gazes into a pink clamshell make-up mirror to light up, displaying a certain genius in the way she flutters her eyelashes.

She chooses her words like a military strategist, uses cigarettes like wands, and always taps her ashes—never flicks.

"Why not?" I argue. "I've been on the bus twice as long as you, and I'm up for it."

"Yes, because you have no bag," she says.

"We'll stash it somewhere."

"We are not stashing my bag anywhere other than the trunk of the car that comes to pick us up."

Of the friends between us in Missoula, three have cars. This is just the way Missoula is. You bundle up and ride your bike in the snow and you like it.

Providence, being who she is, made sure none of our auto-mobile friends are available to receive our call. We do not wait for the tone, and we do not leave a message. Instead, I carry Amelia's bag to the nearest church and we stash it in the bushes.

"You're right, this was a good idea," she says at last, free and easy on the quiet street. In the distance, small mountains cradle the low skyline of Missoula. She says, "I can't wait to see Katie."

"I know. I bet she's huge."

"Tell me the truth," she says. "Do you think Adam is the father?"

"I don't know anymore than you do," I say.

Amelia nods and sets her gaze down the road. "Katie says she's a virgin. That's good enough for me. No father it is." And then she catches me off guard: "Anyway, I heard they broke up."

Broke up? "Katie an Adam? Really?" I can't believe it.

"It's what I heard," she says. "Let's go down to the river!"

"Right now?"

"Yes. Let's go."

Katie and Adam are like a staple of love and fidelity and everything's-gonna-be-okay-ness. The news kind of staggers me.

"It's too late," I say. "I need sleep."

"You sound old," she says.

"Never!"

"You're right. You're like a tall five-year-old."

"The plan is to skip middle age and jump straight from youth to crotchety old asshole."

She gets a kick out of this. Bites my shoulder and growls. "Tell me what you really want," she says.

This is not a question that makes me comfortable.

"I'll go first," she says. "I want to leave my finger-prints everywhere. Touch a million hearts. Never satisfied. Always hungry... Now you."

"Fine," I say. "I want to be a relic."

"Explain."

"I want to change the world, but not right away. Not for hundreds of years. I want them to find my stories in a box sometime in the far off future. And then I want those stories to inspire some crazy new theory no one ever thought of before. To influence the genius who finally figures out time travel. Or that cruising through worm holes is actually pretty easy. Or a brand new way of trying to understand God."

"God is in the river," she says.

"We'll go tomorrow."

"That's all I want to do, okay? At least once before I leave. Stand by the river and look at it. Maybe try to break it."

"Break it?"

"Break it."

"Okay."

"It's not too much to ask."

"No it isn't."

For now it's enough to see our river in the distance. Far below us the Clark Fork claims territory from the city, a canyon of overgrowth climbing up toward this sterile sidewalk that passes for a cliffside path. We move upstream almost at a gallop until Amelia's bad knee starts to hurt. We hold hands. The spade of our arms sways between us. The night is overcast so we pray for stars.

Amelia, who can drift effortlessly from debutante to relentless bitch to supple kitten, recites our prayer: "Dear goddess, thank you for silver grey skies spanning the crumbs of Americana...for sips of pear liquor...for falling into the lap of half-hearted bliss with reflective regret, and si-mul-taneously sending me on a kayak ride into the Grand Canyon of emotion."

She says, "Goddess, teach us to love in spite of pain, to open up rather than shut down, to cultivate hope instead of bitterness, to make madmen into emperors, miracles out of beggars and maestros of the deaf."

She says, "Help us to pay attention to how our feet feel every time we take a step and to notice every sensation in our body all at once. Dear goddess, thank you for deep fried cheddar chunks covered in shredded potatoes. Thank you for the power to change my mind, even if my mind cannot change reality."

She says, "Help me to take responsibility for my inner space, and to give myself permission to feel negative feelings instead of pushing them away. Let your thundering moods entice us to pray without knowing what to say or even looking for the way to say it. To be aware of our breathing. To laugh without getting the joke."

She says, "Dear goddess, please manifest yourself for

us tonight so we can slap you on your goddamn golden goddess ass."

Amelia pauses, makes sure she didn't miss anything, and then turns to me. "How was that?"

"You forgot to mention the stars," I say.

Amelia's laughter, when she realizes she's done something ridiculous, always stops her in her tracks. Her jaw drops and her breath falls out like tiny atom bombs.

She tucks into me like she's trying to hide that gorgeous smile, and she rapid-fires a P.S. over my shoulder: "Dear goddess please stars now, k?"

6.

Amelia and I reach Higgins Street hours after bar time. Downtown is empty. Everyone long stumbled home.

Missoula's layout is pretty simple—Higgins is the spine that holds downtown in place, and all those saloon side streets are her ribs. Her bridge leaps like a pelvis over the river. From there two legs spread southward, starting at the juiciest part of town. One leg sticks straight out draped in a long nylon of businesses, restaurants, banks and malls. The other leg kind of bends at the knee, propping up the University district, and then droops down into a big fat K-Mart/Wal-Mart foot.

The Greyhound Station is on Broadway. Broadway runs into Higgins, which turns into Brooks. Together these streets map out a tour of some of the most asinine roadway decisions in the history of the country.

One of Amelia's friends lives in an apartment above the Old Post. We knock but there is no answer. After a night of drinking, passing out becomes a game of musical couches.

"This would be a lot easier if our busses hadn't been late," she says.

Around 15,000 years ago the valley of Missoula

belonged to some 3,000 square miles of glacial lake. Through the murky tides of change the water left Missoula and never came back. There are not many who can say the same.

Now only the rivers remain. The Blackfoot flows into the Clark Fork, which drives straight through the city westward out of Hellgate canyon, a cleavage of Missoula's branded hills, and into the Bitterroot. This deadly passage brings ice floes in winter and ugly winds in any season. But the moniker "Hellgate" has nothing to do with the weather. It came from the ease with which Indians used the canyon for ambush back in the day.

One of Montana's many statutes leftover from the old days says: *When seven or more Indians are gathered together, they shall be considered a part of a war party.* However, it is illegal to shoot at these groups. More than one Montana law is like the black and white photos of your racist great-grandfather that you can't help gazing on with affection no matter how big of an asshole he was.

There's a house on Spruce street where I can usually just walk in and crash on a couch or a floor. Tonight it's all full up. Two guys still awake by the fireplace take turns hitting a wooden pipe. "Huge party, man," says one through held breath. "You missed it. Pull up a floor if you want."

One look from Amelia and I know she'd rather keep trying. We've both been on a bus for too long not to at least try to find something cushy to sleep on.

I call Missoula home, but I can't ever stay very long. When I'm here I long for oceans, when I'm by the ocean I just want a desert, the desert makes me miss the city, but I see tall buildings and I want my mountains back. So I wander. Deep down I wonder where my nomadic tendencies come from. Maybe I need too much, like I want to be everywhere at once. Or I'm still looking for the perfect spot. The ideal napping place. That patch of ground that fits my ass precisely. But I can't seem to settle in anywhere. My feet start moving and all I can do is hang on.

Amelia and I are halfway across the bridge, right in the cusp of the canyon's prickling breeze, and she asks me, "Are you going to tell me about Vegas?"

"I might."

"You should."

"Maybe I will."

"Do it."

"It wasn't diamonds and roses."

"Stop being evasive," she says. "You're always evasive about your personal life, but this time I have you trapped on a bridge and I can throw you off. So speak. Out with it."

The truth is I moved to Vegas to try and reclaim some continuity in my life. Before Vegas I'd been living out of a truck, owned next to nothing, and I slept in a different state every couple weeks.

"Well, I went down to see this girl—" is what I tell Amelia, which is also true.

"Yes. This unnamed girl you never talk about."

"—and, uh, it didn't work out."

Love and travel both slow down time by zooming in and dissecting each moment, fracturing them into smaller and smaller pieces. Seconds seem like hours. Hours like days.

"Okay," she says. "So why didn't it work out? What did you do? Obviously you didn't come straight home."

"Um."

"Yes?"

"Turns out she was a man."

"I will drown you." Amelia scowls and points suggestively over the guardrail.

For some reason Vegas became a place to rediscover continuity, to escape the cracks in the road and hide away in an endless repetition of identical days. Falling in love was a side effect.

"My heart was broken, okay? What more do you want me to say?"

"I'm sorry." Amelia clutches my elbow, letting me off the hook.

I thought settling down in a strange city would fill in the fractures; I assumed love would smooth over the cracks. But cracks appear everywhere. Now there's one in my chest, and I've followed it back home. Back to the filling station. Back to Missoula. The place where my journeys begin and end. The sanctuary to where I always return and the port from where I always embark. Over and over like the salty cove tide.

"The worst part is she makes me exactly as happy as she makes me miserable," I say.

"You're hopeless," she says.

"Then things got bad."

"How so?"

"I asked her to marry me."

7.

Katie Ludwick once told me that getting a woman is the easiest thing in the world. "Just grab her, and kiss her," she said.

Sounds good on paper. But the time and space between the grab and the kiss is a vast wilderness, easy to get lost, easy to make a split second mistake. The grab is aggressive, teetering on a multitude of violations. If you can transition safely from the grab to the kiss, then violence resolves into passion, and yes, perhaps it is just that simple from there.

But there is no end to the perils of the grab. Even if the lady understands that this grab is a prelude to the kiss, and even if she wants the kiss to happen, she may instinctively resist. Her resistance may break your resolve. Your broken resolve may turn into a shift of the eyes, a stupid, stuttering half-grab awkwardness that leaves you stumbling for the words to explain the grab away before she calls the cops.

The kiss is the only possible justification for the grab.

Nor can you kiss without the grab. It's just too sneaky. And she will never put her face in a position where it can be kissed without some sort of grabby initiator. Sudden kisses unframed by the grab are comical and ridiculous.

A woman opening herself up to a sudden kiss is as likely as a man spreading his legs to an oncoming foot.

"It's easy to talk to women," Katie Ludwick likes to say. "You boys make everything too complicated. Just be like: 'Hi, how are you? I am fine. I like your face. It is pretty. Nice skirt, did you make it? What are you doing? Do you want to be my friend?' "

8.

The world's most recent pregnant virgin lives in an elaborately constructed Victorian ex-brothel. Apartment number nine.

Knock, knock!

Katie is our fifth attempt. If she doesn't answer we'll just have to crash out on the abandoned couch in the alley outside her building.

As we wait Amelia taps her toe on the concrete. She says, "Just because we didn't tell anyone we were coming back does not give any of them an excuse to leave us out in the cold in the middle of the night."

I knock again, softer this time. Katie Ludwick's face emerges on the other side of the glass like a lady who is haunted by rats. Let's call this hypothetical lady "Rat Lady". Katie's hair is bleach-blonde and lilting in fright, all in a tangle so tortuous it can only be a conspiracy of her dreams. Amelia and I smile and wave. Katie scrunches up her eyes and nose and reaches up to scratch her head. I fear her fingers may never escape.

With her other hand she pushes open the old door. It nearly falls off its hinges.

"What are you doing?" asks a sleepy Katie.

"Surprise," I say.

"Hiiiiiii," Katie Ludwick's voice is a six-year-old girl in pajamas reaching out for hugs.

She brings us inside and puts Amelia on the couch. I'm good on the floor.

"Sorry it's so late. It's his fault."

"Whatever, dude," Katie smiles. "I'm going to go back to bed."

"Sleep."

"Sleep."

It's all we want in the whole world, all three of us. Katie's place is a galaxy of blankets, and we drink our fill.

CHAPTER TWO

JACKET

Santa Cruz, CA

The first time I left Montana for the open road I found myself in Santa Cruz, California, destined to fall into the arms of an older woman.

We never spoke a single word to each other.

I met her downtown, headed in the opposite direction through shopping mall doors. I was busy staring at a big mole on my arm and she was busy looking over her shoulder. We nearly collided. I opened my mouth to apologize, and when she did the same I shut my mouth to let her go first. But then she shut her mouth too. Our eyes got all tangled up in a big mess right in the doorway until she smiled and shook it off and walked past me. I followed her back inside and sat across from her in a little café and bought her dinner. We didn't speak all evening. Our precedent was set. Other than fierce moments embroiled in each other's lips, those lips stayed sealed.

We shared her little house just outside of town. She worked in a coffee shop. She had flat fingers and long brown hair, and she coughed in her bathtub through the lungs of a lingering cold.

Sex, not conversation, filled the corners of our days. Between theaters and meals and long walks, passion punctuated the passage of time. Instead of telling me about work she would climb on top of me as if she was Mallory and I was Everest. Instead of asking her to pass me the salt at dinner I'd toss her over the table, and when we were finished she would wink and hand me the pepper.

In the early days of our relationship we made love as if we were planning an expedition to another solar system. As if our entire affair on this planet was training for a future life in which we would be reunited as cosmic revolutionaries destined to depose some galactic despot. We worked up the scheme with our eyes and scratched out blueprints with our teeth. Nothing compares to planning a revolution with your body. The skin is a map. Breath designates time. Fingertips sketch out an itinerary of nonsense.

The old folks told me: *You're wasting your time on this relationship. The two of you never even talk anymore.*

We never talked to begin with, I'd say.

Wasting your youth, they insisted. *You're wasting your youth on pipe dreams and outer space and expeditions and silent romances.*

But isn't that what youth is for—to be wasted?

My youth was like a spring storm in a monastery. It was sex fully dressed in a field of noise where those who have lost their faith come to be baptized into profanity. But when I met my silent barista, life became a calm and steady pool of silent sleep.

One morning I woke up after a good long three weeks with her. Three weeks without sharing a single word. I was thirsty and she walked me to the door. She seemed to know what was coming even though I did not. I'd only meant to go get some orange juice.

She kissed my forehead and unlocked the locks and let me out.

"Goodbye," she said.

1.

I wake up on Katie Ludwick's floor with a fierce longing for bacon, then crawl into Katie's room to make my complaint known. Our host murmurs from beneath kelp-colored quilts, where I can see but one protruding blonde lock of hair, and graciously tells me to go buy some.

As I sit on the corner of Katie's huge bed I notice that Amelia was right. Someone is missing. "Where's Adam?" I ask.

She responds almost before I finish the question, expecting it I guess. "I kicked him out."

Katie Ludwick and Adam Jostler moved in together before I ever left Missoula. We all liked Adam, and approved of him more or less. He was a gentle soul with a heart of gold, overflowing with stories and obscure little facts, like: "almonds are in the peach family", or "snails have been known to sleep for as long as three years." Adam stood half a dozen inches over Katie. He had long blonde hair and a dirty blonde beard that couched his sincere and frequent smile. He seemed to know everyone in town and would spend at least a little quality time with anyone he met. He made a point to recognize something pure and noble in even the most unsavory pieces of shit. And he remembered everyone's name.

"I thought things were good," I say.

Katie sniffles from beneath her blankets. Allergies. "Things were fine until I found out I was full of baby."

"Yeah, I suppose that didn't go over too well."

"Actually, I never told him."

"He doesn't know?"

"I'm sure he knows by now." Katie slowly sticks out a hand and slaps around her end table for Benadryl.

"So why'd you kick him out?"

"The old Adam came back."

When they first started dating Adam was homeless and jobless. Born and raised in Texas, he moved to Butte at fifteen. He wasted a couple restless years there, never finished high school, and then hitchhiked to Missoula. He made friends easily, which was a good thing for him because he spent most nights on someone or other's couch. In the mornings he always picked up the living room, did dishes if there were any to be done, and hit the streets. A professional house guest, Adam never had his own place and he never had a job until he met Katie. He just lived from corner to corner huddling over an old guitar with searing focus, wrapped around that cedar frame like a serpent around its prey.

Then he and Katie fell in love and moved in together. She supported him all summer. They shared a bed, but never went past second base. It isn't that Katie was religious or had a thing about waiting for marriage. She just had a thing about waiting. No one really knew what she was waiting for, least of all Adam—that's what he told me anyway.

Whatever her reasons, he was okay with it. Which was part of why she loved him. Which may have also been part of why she wouldn't have sex with him. Adam once confided in me that their love had become so entwined in the concept of not having sex that the very idea of doing it came with a heavy terror, and he'd reached the point where he wondered if it would ever happen at all.

All of this accounted in part for Katie's toleration of his freeloading. But after five months shouldering the bills, Katie finally put the matriarchal foot down and threatened to kick him the hell out if he didn't find work. So he got a job and stuck with it, and he made rent every month.

"But then he started gambling again," Katie says. "The day I found out about the baby Adam came home and told me he lost all the rent money at Flippers. How do you gamble away 400 dollars in one day?"

"Bad habit for a parent, I guess."

"It just drives me crazy because this is my life partner. I love him. I know I'm supposed to be with him, even now—but he's an asshole. So I just started screaming at him, hitting him. Throwing shit around the room. I told him he had no balls. That he wasn't even a man."

"Ouch."

Katie's head pops out from beneath the blankets. She glares at me. "Well, Jesus!"

"No second chance?" I say.

"This was like, chance number nine," she growls.

She tells me about how she slammed the door on his apology, grabbed her rod and went out fishing. How she stayed on the river for three hours without a single bite. How she randomly recalled Montana's vestigial law that forbids single women from going fishing alone. How she couldn't get the word "caught" out of her head. She wanted to go back to the doctor's office and beat the shit out of the nurse who'd used that term in the first place. She tells me how she drove home and with tears in her eyes ordered Adam to go. He must have expected it because he'd already packed his things. Everything Adam owned fit into one small brown backpack, a duffle bag, and his guitar case. He bore them all like growths on his body, and used his foot to open the door.

Before he left he said, *I'm sorry Katie. And I love you. I guess that's all I can say.*

Yeah well, was all she could say.

Katie blows her nose and tells me how all that Adam left behind was his old black rotary wall phone, which still sat on the coffee table beside Katie's old orange rotary wall phone—two phones that would always belong together.

"I stared at those phones long after he was gone," she says. "Just stared at them, trembling. I remember reaching out and picking up his receiver." I imagine her brushing one finger down the hive of sound holes and then setting it back on its cradle.

Katie changes the subject to keep back tears. I pretend not to notice.

"I'm hungry," she says.

"Me too."

I tell her I'm going shopping, money or no money. I speak the bacon word and her eyes light up.

I try to make Amelia join me on my quest. One tiny hand creeps out from beneath the blanket to point at her purse. I guess it's up to me.

2.

The Holiday gas station across from the Bab's apartments will not have bacon. I know this as surely as I know I must find the stuff and eat it, or die trying. Eight blocks away is a local grocery known to my clan by a straight reading of its acronym: OSFF (pronounced oss-uh-fuff).

The simple and potent pleasure of walking down a Missoula street late in the morning hits me by the second block. It is not a pleasure you can find in either the city or the woods, but only in some place precisely in-between. Neither will you find it in a brochure, a bottle, or a book. Along ruptured sidewalks, sunlight scatters, torn into strips by a translucent canopy of Ash leaves. Eccentric houses unroll shaggy lawns, sleeping fences, and the remains of last week's garage sale. No two blocks are alike. If it's continuity you seek, leave it to the sidewalks, or the birdsong, or the rare and steady beat of passing cars. Walking through Missoula is the pleasure of slipping from nowhere to somewhere—though it may be the other way around, you don't know for sure, and in such carefree ignorance you swallow the secret whole.

I am struck by how in certain brief moments, in certain square feet of town, Missoula can smell exactly like the wilderness. I have been away for too long. My pallet is cleared, and today, for as long as I can make it last, I'll soak up the good parts of this intoxicating town, and ignore the fact that she never fails to leave a hangover.

OSFF's automatic doors slide open. My thundering heart drags me straight to the bacon aisle. Yes, picture it—an aisle full of bacon. I dig through the bulging bacon bin, peeking behind the secret nativity-calendar flaps for the precise ratio of fat to meat that will fully justify the dollar eighty-eight I am about to spend. It is Amelia's money, bless her soul, and I will not squander this gift.

So many lovely items assail my journey to the checkout. A six pack of local micro brew for four dollars! Candy bars in a cardboard display bin, five for a dollar— that's right. OSFF, I could kiss you. Still, all I'm after this morning is bacon and all I can afford is bacon, and bacon is all I get. No bag, thanks. Who can't carry a package of bacon without a bag?

The last time I shopped at OSFF was only days before I fled Missoula for the coast on the long, twisty journey that would ultimately bring me to Vegas. I'd only come in for a sandwich, but I ended up wandering around the aisles for two hours. Carrying that sandwich the whole time. At first I thought I wanted something else, something to accompany the sandwich. Nothing looked good. Sometimes a thing would start to look good until I reached toward it or touched the packaging, but then I would recoil and move to a new aisle. Two hours of this.

That's when I knew I had to leave. In leaving Missoula, I learned to want Missoula back again, and all other mute desires rekindled within me.

3.

Returning to Katie's building I trickle down the steps and open the door. A blast of bacon scented girl slaps me up the nose, along with familiar sizzles. There stands Katie Ludwick in the kitchen, gristly fork in hand, meditating upon her sacred searing strips.

"You had bacon the whole time," I gawk.

"Dude, I always have bacon."

"Why didn't you say so?"

"I forgot."

"You forgot you always have it?"

I throw the new package in the fridge with the remains of the frying package, the reserve package, and the package that's been sitting unopened for weeks.

Katie looks so beautiful standing there in smeared pajama bottoms and bulging tank top. A slim strip of belly button flesh peeks out above her waistband.

When Katie Ludwick was seventeen she dreamed of starting a revolution. She told me she'd never get married or have kids. She said: "Single women without babies are the most powerful creatures on the planet. Men of all ages find them attractive; every woman secretly wants to be them. Every ounce of passion and love that would otherwise go to a child can go to changing the world. Mothers are narrow, single-minded creatures. When you have a baby that's all you care about. The world doesn't matter anymore except in relation to your own stupid kid. Everyone else can go to hell as long as your baby is okay. But the world doesn't need more fragmented love," she said. "I want to create more independence, not more need. I want to change the world, dammit."

Like most people, Katie Ludwick is made up of two contradictory selves. On one hand there's the slovenly Katie. This Katie sleeps past noon and then continues to lie in bed watching video-recorded soap operas after she wakes up. This Katie spends her days wandering through town, fishing the rivers, going to coffee shops and visiting friends.

Then there's Katie the rabid artist. When the mood strikes her this Katie will hole up in her studio for days, painting, drawing, cutting and taping. Her art isn't anything your run-of-the-mill critic would call great, but it possesses the kind of wild imagination and raw honesty that cannot be learned. She makes collages like she's cutting out pieces of her soul. Her paintings are mad stews of dark, blended colors and shuddering images, often textured with trinkets and bits of glass. She also makes these Frankenstein grotesques out of creepy old dolls and other random toys.

One time we took an old typewriter out to the woods and blew it all to hell with a shotgun. Katie brought the pieces back home and made a sculpture. She said, "Sometimes you have to tear a thing apart so that its soul can get out."

Katie also draws cartoon stick figures. These are my favorite. They look like little kid drawings, but somehow this huge depth of expression and meaning flies out from between the skinny lines. And they're hilarious.

My favorite is a quick pencil drawing of two deformed little monsters. A copy of this sketch still lives on a piece of orange paper in a tiny corner of my backpack. One of the creatures says, "Hello, alien," and the other replies, "Hello, freak". She also has this sketch of three monsters, the littlest of whom tells the others to "quit looking drunk."

When I consider Katie's virgin pregnancy I always think of her art. She brings things into existence with natural ease. Her lazy-self teams up with her artistic-self, and her best work seems to come from her slightest efforts. She wills these things into existence with an afterthought, like pulling a rabbit out of a hat. Maybe her fetus came from the same place.

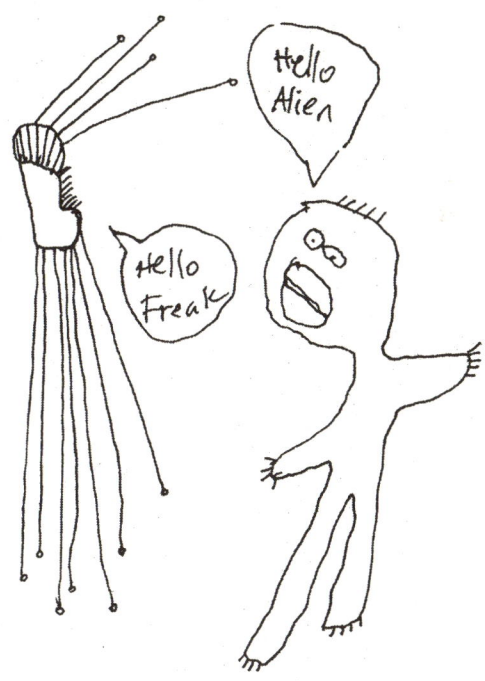

4.

"Or maybe you were abducted—you know, by aliens. Maybe you're a host."

She wrinkles up her forehead and frowns when I say this, as she does with most of my suggestions.

"So I'm going to have an alien baby?" she says.

"Well it wouldn't necessarily be a bad thing—I mean, these aliens would have to be pretty smart to pull it off. It'd be a superhuman child, genetically advanced. Maybe he'll lead humanity into the stars."

"She."

"What?"

"She. She's a girl."

"You got an ultrasound?"

Katie stabs a strip of bacon. "No. I just know."

The way she looks at me now reminds me of a tired old sea turtle, 200 years old and ready for its next incarnation.

"I read about this old sea turtle who raised a group of orphan hippos," I say.

"No shit?"

"No shit."

I pull a shrieking teakettle off the stove and hunt around for cups.

"I want to go to a foreign country," Katie says. "And when I get there I'll go around saying blah blah blah to people on the street and nobody will know the difference."

This feels like the perfect moment to ask, "Where's my jacket?"

"What jacket?"

"My torn up blue jacket—the boxing jacket. The infamous jacket of utter coziness. What do you mean, *what jacket?*"

"That's my jacket," she says.

"I'm reclaiming it. Where is it?"

She holds the fork up to my face, glistening pig flesh scrolling at the corners. "I lent it to my brother. Here eat this."

"I haven't seen him wear that jacket since high school." I bite the bacon. It is, in fact, delicious.

"Oh yeah. It was his jacket first. I almost forgot."

"It's my jacket," I say. "He gave it to me."

"He gave it to me before he gave it to you," Katie counters. "Here, eat this."

Meanwhile, Amelia is in the living room trying on all of Katie's clothes.

"What are you doing?" I ask.

"I'm trying on all of Katie's clothes. Someone talked me into ditching my bag last night."

"Well, that looks good," I say.

Amelia drowns a yellow Dixie's Diner shirt beneath a hulking black hoodie. "It looks good on Katie. Not on me."

As Amelia strips back down to her underwear she shouts, "How can you be pregnant if you're a virgin?"

"Word on the street is you have to be one or the other," I add.

Katie's voice crawls back from the kitchen. "You guys are geniuses."

Amelia climbs into a pair of stained Carhartts and says, "Well, are you pregnant or aren't you?"

"Obviously."

"And you're really a virgin."

"Yes."

"You and Adam seriously never had sex?"

Katie's head pokes around the corner. She wields her fork like a trident. "I just wasn't ready," she says.

"Are you sure he didn't—you know...like, when you were drunk or passed out or something?"

"No," Katie gives us one of her patented death glares. "Adam would never do that. Anyway, the doctor checked me out. I'm intact."

"Didn't the doctor have a theory?"

"I could tell she didn't want to think about it. She acted like it was no big deal."

"I'm sure she's confident the facts will eventually yield to common sense," I say.

Katie's situation reminds me of the French film, Léolo. Léolo believed that his own conception resulted from his mother falling into a cart of inseminated tomatoes.

Back down to nothing but matching purple bra and panties, Amelia rushes to the bathroom. As she passes by Katie she opens her mouth and Katie delivers the bacon. Bathroom door slams.

As Katie tends to her sizzling stove I'm left in the living room staring out the windows. After a minute I hear the click of a burner shutting off. Katie shuffles up beside me, carying a scuffed-up water bottle and a yellow apple.

"Now I know why people have sex," she says.

"Oh yeah?"

"So when they get knocked up, even if they've been slutting around with the entire congregation, at least they can say: the father is one of these guys. Maybe they don't know who and maybe they really don't care, but at least he's someone. But I don't get to do that. Instead, I have to say there is no father, and put up with the kind of cross examination you guys are giving me now."

She tells me that she considered having sex with Adam just to avoid confusion, but she'd already kicked him out of the house. She'd told him not to call her, to just leave her alone. Wouldn't have been any big deal if she weren't still in love with him.

"I wonder what he thinks," I say.

"I'm sure he thinks I cheated on him. Which is fine, because that probably makes him feel better about the breakup." Katie cradles her water bottle to her breast. Practicing, I reckon.

The bathroom door flies open. Amelia emerges in a loose bathrobe, a pair of Pokemon PJs, and a blue T-shirt. "This will have to do," she says.

"There's something called parthenogenesis," I tell Katie. "I looked it up. It's a form of reproduction without fertilization. It occurs naturally sometimes with aphids, bees, scorpions, fish. Even a few birds I think."

"I'm not a fish," Katie Ludwick says.

"Yeah, I know." The challenge of finding ways to make sense of her situation surpasses my abilities. I say, "Just think about all the virgin births in mythology. Some beautiful examples. Not counting the obvious, take Lao Tzu for instance. Conceived when his mother saw a falling star. That's a nice story."

"Can we not talk about this anymore?" Katie groans.

Amelia leans over last night's makeshift bed and gathers up all the shrapnel from around where she dropped her purse. "Do you have a coat? I need a coat. I'm a coat person."

"What about the coat you were wearing last night?"

"Does it look like last night to you?"

"I'll go get your bag," I say.

"No, I've got a ride coming. Here, give me hugs. I'm going outside." Amelia bounces over a pile of jeans and wraps her arms around my neck. Her perfume smells almost comical amidst the fat frying ambiance. She squeezes me stork-like, one foot dangling in the air.

Out she goes, cigarettes in hand, to wait in the alley. Out of my life as quick as she came in. Always that girl is walking away, following whatever dot her eyes have affixed upon the horizon, always leaving me with words on my lips. For the life of me I don't know what those words are.

5.

At Katie's request I put on some music. Donovan is morning music. Breakfast-making music. *Colors, Catch the Wind, Season of the Witch*. When the bacon is ready we segue into the Ramones. We sit side-by-side on the couch and crunch leathery pig flesh to the hiss of a dying cassette tape.

"Welcome home," Katie says.

"Thanks," I say. "How've you been?"

"Fat."

"You look good."

"I'm glowing, apparently."

"Where's your brother?"

Katie laughs. "You really want that jacket."

"Yes."

"I don't know. He's probably at Flippers."

When I leave, Amelia is still outside waiting. I catch her by the elbow on the stairs. Her toes tap the concrete and I touch her arm. She stops and turns and does not speak. Her mind is full of complicated games that I can only crash through in strange sidewalk moments. She takes one step back toward me. Without really knowing why, I lean in to deliver a kiss. She follows my lead for a split second, but then her head darts away gazing down like a street lamp at my blemished brown boots.

"Hmm," she says.

"What?"

"Just, hmm."

She pulls out a cigarette and lights it with a pink lighter. I notice speckled fingernail polish for the first time. "I am a broken machine. Let's go to the river," she says.

"Now?"

"Yes. No. YES!"

I glance down the alley at the Flippers Casino sign. My jacket is only yards away, I'm sure of it!

"No," she says. "My ride will be here any minute."

I feign a dramatic tone. "We'd never make it anyway."

"It's only two blocks away," she pouts. "I can smell it. Let's go. We can play break the river."

"What's that?"

"You stand in the river with a rock or a tree branch or whatever, and you smash it. You try to break off pieces of the river. First person to break the river in half wins."

"This is an actual game?"

"Sometimes it's important to do something completely futile," she says.

"Find me later tonight. We'll go."

Amelia glances up with eyes popping fireworks. "I will find you," she says, "and you can tell me all about your torrid affair with Vegas girl."

Las Vegas, NV

I first met her under the gasp of a clear winter night. I was still unfamiliar with the city, so I was half trying to find my way back to my apartment and half trying to identify the few stars peeking through the eerie magenta Vegas haze. She was kneeling down in the street and I didn't see her at all. I nearly tripped over her legs. Then I tried to step around her like she was road construction.

"Hey, listen to this," she said. Her head was sideways on the ground, earlobe caressing a manhole cover. "Down here."

I glanced around, clearing my throat.

"Water," she said.

I stood there without words. I could tell she was dead sexy, even in the dark.

"You can't hear it from up there. Come down on the ground."

I crouched down beside her, tilted my head, and I heard it. Gushing running dirty sewer water. I'd never listened to the sounds beneath the streets before, never bothered to try. She stared at me with the jewel of her eyes as we knelt crook-headed and flat on the iron platter, noses inches apart. She beamed at the sound, eyes darting back and forth like an optical lens across a CD. I smiled at her. Couldn't have stopped if I'd wanted to. "People live down there," she whispered.

"What people?" I whispered back, conforming to whisper's infection.

"Homeless. The mayor says we don't have any, but that's because he hides them away. They all live underground."

"Oh." We knelt there for a long time, listening, staring, silently planning out our next few months together, months that became a mythology of opposites in the spaces between words. By the following week we were inseparable. Even the nights we spent apart were bound by phone calls, letters, schemes to impress and surprise the other, agreements to both stare up at the moon at such and such a time.

I once delivered a box full of bouncy balls to her door with instructions to tip them all at once down a hill.

She disguised herself with a short blonde wig and glasses, set me on a chase through the city, clue after clue, until I found her in a bakery, hiding behind a newspaper like some sort of Russian agent in an old spy movie.

We traded dreams. I wrote her stories. She drew me pictures. I gave her baths and cooked her dinner. She found it all delicious and climbed over piles of dishes to cling to my ribs. She's the only woman I thought maybe I could have babies with.

I'd have bet every casino on the Strip it would never end.

6.

Flippers Casino isn't even a block away from Katie's house. Just kitty-corner across the alley. Somehow I still manage to see someone I know before I reach the parking lot. It has begun. They will be popping up everywhere now. Who knows how many I'll meet at Flips. In a town of people who know people, Flippers is a veritable den of everybody who knows everybody.

This one is William. We've been friends since high school. Will is on his way to get today's ration of coffee and cigarettes. When he spots me his eyes widen through his glasses, and as he comes to a theatrical stop his arms spring up to point me into existence.

"You're back!"

"Yes."

"So, um..."

"Flippers."

"Okay, I'll be right there, just have to get coffee," and he dashes off.

Describing Flippers is as hard as describing my mom. Try describing your mom and you'll see what I mean. She's too familiar to begin breaking her into pieces, and it's almost uncomfortable to try. All I can say is that Flippers is nothing if not dim. Thin strips of neon weave a highway between flashing beer signs. The jukebox by the door provides most of the illumination, along with whatever blinky lights escape from the keno machines.

I grab the handle, do not turn it, and tug. Years ago someone broke the latch and it stayed that way for so long that when Flippers' management finally got around to fixing it none of the regulars could figure out what to do. Every single one of us who attempted entry after the fix, resorting to our habitual pulling or pushing, would—I swear to God—freeze for a moment of total panic, wondering if either a) Flippers had shut down, or b) we were trapped inside forever. Depending on which side of the door we stood. And no one learned better. Drunkenness thrives on habit. Instinct shoves its way past coordination and rational thought, insisting that if it can't find the way no one can. And no one thought to use the handle. Eventually we'd just bang on the door until a bartender let us in. It happened all the time. Finally management decided they'd better just break the latch again, and they did, and thank God for that.

And so, pulling without twisting, I enter a land of keno machines, cheap wine, and tall tables.

Dennis works behind the bar, grinning at me from the other side of his Groucho mustache. I don't think I've ever seen that man's lips. Dennis' mustache is a pair of eight-inch forearms folded across a barrel chest. Without that mustache I'd put Dennis at about five-foot-six. With it, he's six-foot-nine.

"Hi Josh!"

He buys me a beer just for being gone so long and asks me about my trip. Some small talk ensues, and meanwhile a few other people I know pass by and say hello. I glance over to the keno machines. I can hear the sound of numbers flashing, I can see the old ladies melting into their chairs, fixated upon glowing screens like those podlings from the Dark Crystal parting with their essence.

"Is Ludwick here?"

"Yeah he's over there somewhere losin' money," Dennis says.

"Did he have a jacket on?" I ask this for drama's sake, and to heighten my own anticipation. "It's sort of a light blue denim boxer's jacket."

"What's a boxer's jacket?"

"Is he wearing any jacket at all?" Dennis has no idea. He laughs at me and says maybe.

7.

I creep among the machines and the regulars. Flippers houses some dusty old gems. The usual crowd takes pride in their backwoods alcohol-fueled inheritance, and they remain humble about the literacy and insight they've acquired in spite of it.

Missoulians are a curious breed. Out here you can throw a rock in a crowd and good odds you'll hit one of the metal-loving neo-hippie deer-hunting earth-firster redneck liberal vegans who serve up modern dance with their football. The kind who own multiple handguns and still believe in gun control; who find homosexuality disgusting, but will fight to defend gay marriage; who don't really buy into global warming, but realize alternative energy is still a goddamn smart idea; who think we sure as hell should have bombed someone after 9/11, but why Iraq for Chrissakes?!

Smoke rises from an ashtray near an empty wine glass at the far end of the room. Dean has keno-vision and does not see me approach. He is wearing a black T-shirt, no jacket. I flank him and see the glowing image of the machine miniaturized onto his glasses.

I watch him lose a few credits and then I say, "The secret is to bet up just before you win."

"I'm trying," Dean replies without moving. He raises his bet and clicks. Numbers flash and he gets three out of seven. Not good enough.

"Don't you have these things figured out yet?"

"I figured out they take in more than they pay out."

"And yet you keep playing."

"Yes. I'm a machine that pays out more than I take in."

"Sounds like a match made in heaven," I say.

"Hey did I tell you what happened to me the other day?"

This is how things are with me and Dean. I've been away for months, but instead of saying, *Wow! Welcome home. How was your trip?* he dives into a story about his day. C.S. Lewis once wrote that the mark of true friendship is when two people, separated for any number of months or years, can reunite as if no time has passed at all. The conversation picks up right where it left off.

He's shaved his head since I last saw him. A hint of hair just starting to grow back in. His shrubby red beard hangs off freckled cheeks and nestles below his thin lips like an old grandpa cradling a remote control.

"Zo-zee-zaz," says Dean, wiggling his fingers at the screen. He places his bet.

"What's that," I ask, "some sort of magic spell?"

"Christian magic. Zozezaz," he repeats, this time with extra flamboyance. "A Gnostic invocation to elude alien overlords who try to block the soul's ascent to the transcendent God."

"And it works on keno?"

"The damned machines impede my journey! I say Zozezaz, brother! Look at that. Twenty credits. You have to use the right numbers, though. See, 11, 19, 33, and 49 were all hits."

"Obviously."

"You should see the Coptic diagrams," says Dean. "They look like ancient electrical schematics."

"You were going to tell me about your day."

"Oh yeah," Dean picks new numbers. "So I was walking across the bridge," he says. "I saw an osprey swoop down into the river to grab a fish. Just then I passed a bum. He asked me for change. I gave him everything I had—something like two bucks—and I said, *Did you see the osprey?* Guess what he said."

"I have no idea"

"He said, *I baptize you in the name of the fish,* and then he threw all my money over the railing. We both leaned over and watched it hit the water."

This kind of thing happens to Dean all the time. Sometimes I wonder if he just imagines it. Sometimes Dean wonders the same thing.

"Weird," I say. "Then what?"

"Then we went our separate ways."

"And you came to Flippers and won fifty bucks?"

"No," he says. "I didn't have any money left. I just went home."

"That's kind of anti-climactic."

"Wrong. Backward. The whole story is one free-falling climax!"

I took our glasses up to the bar for refills, free to gamblers. When I returned, Dean was up to over two hundred nickels.

8.

Dean lives in a nebulous zone between mastery over his surroundings and complete dissociation with reality. He married a girl once, a few years back. They'd dated for over a year, then they got married and divorced three months later. They moved out to Portland after the wedding and that's where everything fell to shit. Dean said she changed on a dime, like someone flipped a switch, or the wedding ring severed a crucial psychic tripwire. Their relationship disintegrated within weeks, but he stayed on in the apartment with her and her new boyfriend until he could afford to move back home. The boyfriend moved in and Dean moved to the couch. Sometimes they jammed together on guitars. "He was pretty cool," Dean said.

By the time he moved back to Missoula Dean was seeing prophecies and conspiracies everywhere. There's no doubt he'd gone over the edge emotionally, and maybe the rational side of his brain—which had always managed to dig his best battlefield trenches—was overcompensating.

Delusions and false memories infiltrated his daily life. Something like an overdrive of the imagination, or a subconscious attempt to construct an alternate reality to the one he'd lived through. Pieces of his stories were probably true, and parts of them probably weren't. For a while he believed that he was under FBI surveillance. Later Dean got it into his head that he was the "Red Brother" of Hopi prophecy—that it was his job to go to the southwest and save the world. He took a bus to Arizona, stayed with the Hopi until they told him to go home. Nothing dramatic happened. No gathering of the masses, no flashes of insight, no car chases. He went, he told them he was on a mission, and he came home.

Even so, I can't shake the feeling that maybe he did save the world. You can't really prove he didn't, and well, we're all still here.

9.

"Where's my jacket?" I ask.

"What jacket," Dean says.

"The old comfy blue one. Katie said she gave it to you."

"Um...I think it's at home."

"Cash out and buy us some fries," I say.

Dean wavers. He doesn't like to walk away until he's either doubled his money or lost it all.

Up walks Will, returning with coffee to rescue Dean from this moral dilemma. Will's a handsome chap with short dark hair and the most heightened sense of wonder I have ever known. Kids in high school labeled Will a computer geek because they didn't know any better. Truth is, he isn't nearly as excited about computers as he is about the things you can do with them.

"I have returned! You're gambling?"

"He's gambling. I'm starving."

"Don't go anywhere. I'm getting a drink."

Dean keeps up the keno, kicking into high gear. He's betting the maximum and his credits avalanche toward zero. Then he hits five out of seven and the rapid clicks of victory run his numbers back up to equilibrium.

"So you saw my sister?" Dean asks.

"Yeah, I crashed there last night."

"How's she doing?"

"She looks like she's about to pop," I say.

"That's what she gets for staying a virgin so long."

"Your dad should have warned her about that."

Dean yawns into a stretch, looks like he's about to cash out, thinks better of it, and bets big.

I say, "Pregnancy suits her. She looks good."

"Who's pregnant?" Will bounces back with a cold mug of Roscoe's Ale. Froth sparkles on his lips, thickening up a perpetual five o'clock shadow.

"Katie."

Will suspends the moment by sneezing into the breast of his jacket. A single sniffle follows, and he says, "Katie's pregnant?"

"Yep."

"Why didn't I know this? Since when?"

"About eight months," says Dean.

"I'm out of the loop," says Will.

"Dean thinks it's the second coming of Christ."

"Maybe," Dean corrected. "Odds are the second Christ was already aborted."

"I thought Jesus was supposed to return full-grown and ready for a fight."

"What if the Antichrist was aborted?"

"That would put a wrinkle in the pro-life movement."

"I can see the headlines: *Abortion saves the Universe*."

Dean says, "Okay, I'm done." He's run all those credits down to nothing. Well, almost nothing. He cashes out with a single credit, and places the ticket in front of the buzzing blue screen.

"For luck," he says.

10.

We emerge from the Flippers dungeon into the bright, squinting light of noon and settle into three plastic patio chairs. The conversation continues apocalyptically onward. I feel a welling joy at the bliss that comes from trying to puzzle out the inscrutable. I've been gone too long from other minds, trapped too deeply within the succubus of pacing and useless thoughts.

Dean begins: "If the world is a sequence of orderly events, like an interconnected Rube Goldberg machine tumbling forth from a precise, premeditated configuration, then the ending must be inherent in the beginning. Encoded, if you will—"

"I will," I say.

"No," William puns, "*I* Will."

"—Like the way DNA unfolds into a living organism."

Will jumps in with more detail. "Right. A gene interacts with its environment to produce observable phenotypes—" He interrupts himself with one lonely, violent hiccup. Will is the only man I've ever met whose hiccups are isolated rather than chronic: here a random antisocial hiccup dripping with paranoia, there a sociopath sniper hiccup in a bell tower. He continues,

"—and these are epiphenomenon you'll never actually find one-to-one correspondences to in the DNA."

As Will recites the leapfrogging word *epiphenomenon*, I wonder how such syllables ever wound up in his brain.

Across the parking lot stands the greatest low-budget apartment complex in town, a flop palace for starving artists and fizzling musicians. I crashed there for a few months the first time I dropped out of college, sleeping on a tiny orange air mattress in the corner of a friend's room. Glancing now at all the little trinkets and candles perched on the rows of windowsills, the strings of beads and slung tie-died tapestries, I am struck by how familiar it all seems. All those default decorations of life straight out of high school, when you're just learning how to take care of yourself, before you have the first clue what you really want.

"Exactly," Dean stabs a finger into the air. "And since our entire lives are ultimately reducible to a long sequence of only four unique molecules, mightn't the end of civilization be just so encoded in the ancient kabalas and prophecies of madmen?"

Lately I've felt like I'm stuck right on the edge of what I want. Like up to this very moment I've been living a knock-off version of my dreams.

Dean continues, "It could happen. Self-fulfilling prophecy. Fanatics and politicians. Too much power in the hands of someone who thinks they're the voice of God. Someone who reads every current event into some old text."

Will nods. He leans down to yank a yellow-striped dress sock up over his shin. "They believe in Armageddon, and so they try to bring it about."

Lately I feel less like an entity and more like a pile of parts, a sequence of gears. Dean, despite delusional segues, has always been just the opposite, fundamentally unchangeable. I sometimes think Dean will spend the rest of his life in Missoula, hunched over a desk conducting intricate patterns in ink, tracing my orbits as I bounce around the world.

"Are we saying the world can't end on its own?"

Will diverts the subject: "Could it have *begun* on its own?"

I love to watch them fence this way.

Dean gets that tone in his voice like he intended this turn in the conversation all along. "Of course. The world couldn't help but begin."

Lately I've come to realize that everything I want to know about, I know in fragments. Because my life is a jigsaw puzzle where, even if everything gets set down in the right order, none of the pieces touch. An illusion of happiness, vapid reflections on the surface of a pond, haggard by ripples, wrinkles. Old age is just an afternoon nap away. Then where will I be? Will I be happy after all the chasing? Sitting on the porch with a handful of disjointed dreams.

"What do you mean?" Will asks—his mouth agape, anticipating a sneeze that never unfolds.

"Isn't it obvious? Okay, answer this: what was here before the universe?"

"God?" says Will.

"Another universe?" I try.

Dean's eyebrows buckle. Will has caught him off-guard. He turns in his chair. "God? I thought you were an atheist."

Will stares longingly into his empty pint glass, watching the foam slake down the sides. "So what if I am? Maybe I'm an atheist who believes in God."

Thinking back, I'm pretty sure this edge I'm on has

been right there in front of me the whole time. Like the world's horizon, or a mirage that moves forward when you move forward and stops when you stop. Happiness is the carrot dangling from a stick fused to your spine, and chasing it is as productive as trying to jump out of your own shadow.

Dean laughs, "Out West there's not much difference between those who believe in God and those who don't."

Unless chasing happiness *is* happiness...

"Jesus was an atheist, you know."

"You should make it your life's mission to prove that."

"Maybe I will."

Sandwiched between the mystic and the scientist, I adopt the role of keeping things on track. "Okay let's get back to this theory that the world couldn't help but begin."

"Right," Dean continues. He leaps to his feet and begins to pace. "It's simple. Trace backward to the void. Nothingness—right? Well, it's no great leap to get from nothing to something."

"How so?"

Maybe true happiness is a well-aged disappointment that you drink when you're old.

"Easy. If there's nothing existing, then there's nothing to stop things from popping into existence. No laws of physics, no barriers, no forces, no fences. Not even logic."

Will thinks it over. "So, if nothing; therefore something—is that what you're saying?"

Maybe true happiness comes not from getting what you want; but from wanting what you don't really want, and then not getting it.

"Exactly," Dean rakes four fingers through the red tentacles of his beard. "Of course, once things start existing, then you quickly build up a system of limitations. The rules start to congeal. You get things that won't let any other things take up the same space. You get laws of motion and interaction. By the time you reach recorded history it's hard to come up with anything really new."

Will ponders this and slurps down the final few gathering drops of beer.

Whatever my younger self wanted, or thought he wanted living in the squalor of that apartment across the alley, I've long forgotten. But whatever it was, I don't think I got it—and I'm just going to go ahead and thank my lucky stars for that.

"There's supposed to be a party tonight somewhere," Dean says.

"Where?"

"Not sure. I just heard a rumor."

"Music?"

"Probably."

"And girls?"

"Of course," Dean says.

"Sounds wild."

I want to go. I want to chase what I don't want—

"It's something to do."

—and not get it.

11.

We circle a few more blocks, tell some jokes, and pose new riddles we've heard. I walk back to Katie's house after an embarrassing four straight losses to Will's superior riddle medicine. Dean goes the other way, on a quest for medicine of his own. He promises to bring my jacket by later.

Katie's door is unlocked, but the place is empty. She's left a note: *Gone to the doctor. Do whatever you want. Love, Katie.*

Whatever I want, huh? There are a thousand things to do in Missoula with or without money, but I don't feel like being out anymore. Katie's den of slovenly delight clutches at me like a child digging through a pile of puppies. The sink is full of sleeping grimy dishes. The floor is an archipelago of dirty clothes, quilts, and art supplies.

I spot a spatula poking out between couch cushions. I liberate it with one swift tug, recalling Excalibur, and notice it is clean. How a clean spatula got from the kitchen to the couch I will never know. I hold it up to the light. One corner has melted flat from careless usage, a grotesque plastic tumor, a hunchback, a spot of leprosy. I feel its self-conscious gaze. Oh spatula, you are devastated and deformed, but still as useful as ever. Shall I aspire to impart unto you the secrets of space and time?

I explain to the spatula that of all the things Katie and I share, the deepest connection is this: we both make a point of trusting the Universe to take care of us. I can't count how many times money has arrived out of the blue precisely when it was needed, or how often food seemed to barrel down the street in search of some hunger to fill. I know my parents used to live this way, too. At some point you stop—I guess when the novelty wears off, or when you decide it's just luck and your number's about to come up.

"But until then, spatula," I say, "there's magic ripe for the grabbin'. It's in the air and it's attracted to motion." Somehow this cosmic medicine prefers a moving target. Stick your head out of a car window and you'll feel a wind, even on the calmest of days. "It's a Jesus lifestyle, spatula. *The son of man has no place to lay his head.* He was a nomad who thought people should live in the moment. I've met more Atheists on the road living like the man and not even realizing it; and more Christians who've devoted their lives to securing a luxurious place to lay their heads." They live by balance-books, nine-to-fives, and holiday vacations, trapped in schedules and budgets while they sport their WWJD bracelets. But Jesus said not to worry about tomorrow. Tomorrow will take care of itself. "Don't bury your head in the future, spatula!" I shout, "Don't fret about heaven and eternal salvation—for eternity is here and salvation is now, not in some abstract tomorrow waiting a ways off down the line. Faith does not save you; faith *is* salvation. Love does not get us into heaven; love *is* heaven. To love and hope and believe is to enter immediately through the gates. Don't confuse the country for the passport, spatula. Don't mistake the map for the territory. Heaven runs parallel to all premeditated paths. Go one step out of your way to help a stranger and you're there. You've transcended time and space and self. What sort of nebulous eternal realm can compete with that?"

The spatula does not reply. It must be thinking the question over very hard. I walk to Katie's desk and push the flat of the spatula against a disheveled stack of papers. I scramble them up a bit. The stack seems to be in no better or worse order than before.

"Okay, spatula, forget the spiritual side. Just look at it from a practical point of view. An empty wallet is not that bad. Hell, being broke is actually pretty good these days. Most Americans are in debt, and compared to a big fat debt zero is a pretty big number."

People end up in debt out of fear that they will one day have nothing. But having nothing is so damned cheap.

I think this is why you find the one-day-at-a-time lifestyle in so many unexpected places: folks out on the road, hitchhiking, biking, walking, jostling along in old beat-up cars with great mileage. They realize the universe is full of stuff, and you can go out and open your mouth wide, and as long as you keep walking, the rain will fall in. It's like Dean's theory of creation. The more you have, the less you're open to receive. Possessions ultimately dispossess. Bound and saddled you can no longer move fluidly through a fluid world.

Spatula and I circle the room, blessing objects with a light touch from his gnarled melty corner. We bless a baby doll. Katie has blackened in her eyes, dreaded out her hair, and stapled trinkets to her arms. The front end of a Tonka truck emerges from her stomach. We bless a stuffed moose and a rotting avocado. Each blessed object gets a front row seat on the couch. I've lined them all up, dolls, toys, journals, plates, records, stamps, toothpaste, a bottle of witch hazel, a ball of string. Spatula understands now. He has seen the light, and together we propound our holy sermon.

"The people of earth never were cut out for this sedentary lifestyle," I explain. "Millions of years of evolution, fine tuning these beautiful nomadic legs, and in less than two hundred years we've folded them up and put them away under our laptops. We weren't meant to sit in chairs and hide in holes. The wanderer's legacy is too strong, too deeply rooted in the DNA, and it will roam whether we like it or not, if not physically then psychologically. If we don't move our legs, that spirit will smoke and spin and whirl like a clutched axle. The dislodged gears burning up and burning out!"

But what can we do? There's already so many of us, and more coming down the pipelines every minute. Won't be long until we top ten billion. We're running out of room fast. Do we just pack tighter and tighter? Try to sit more still? Or is it possible to maintain momentum in some sort of coordinated way?

My audience hangs on every word. "We need a new method," I proclaim. "Rugged individualism may have worked out okay on the frontier, but we humans we're fresh out of frontiers. The world washed us westward until we ran into the farther shore, and then all the rules changed. The system fed back in on itself. We didn't hit the launch in time." I keep brushing shoulders with old men running on grumpy because there's no more wilderness to steal, stockpiling guns as if any arsenal could protect them from the information infrastructure.

Times change. And what I like about Missoula is how she tries to balance on the cusp of change without letting herself drown in it. One foot forward, ready to adapt, one foot firmly rooted where we came from. Missoula is a filter for letting through all the good parts of our steel-nosed pioneer legacy, while driving back the tides of inertia that tend to keep what were once great ideas chugging along past the point of usefulness.

From the couch my congregation nods and smiles as the spirit fills their plastic nooks and ceramic bits. "I have to tell you, my brothers and sisters, I, too, feel the stale rust seeping in. The dread of motion, the dread of standing still. Sometimes I can't tell which is which and it scares me out of my mind. What if the doors fly open against my will—and rather than me going out, something else comes in? What if I stay in one place too long and the rest of the world rushes on without me? What if in my haste it dissolves into nothingness...as if it all weren't already some dream."

And what the hell would I do, anyway, if I ever found a place suitable to stay put? Would I settle down? Cook breakfast? Sleep under the stars? Find a woman? Build a cabin? Grow old? Die? Do we spend our whole lives looking for that perfect view overlooking some ideal patch of grass on which to settle in and sink slowly beneath the weeds? The rush of the wind, a gentle rain. These icons of what it means to have been alive in a world. Surrounded by the trinkets of our past, the towers of unopened boxes packed tight with so many memorable days never again brought to mind. Then at last, tucked-in best as can be, to etch that moment onto a gravestone and experience nothing more forever.

My arm drops to my side. The spatula slips from my grasp, and finds a new home on the floor between a beanbag chair and a milk crate. I don't even remember what point I was trying to make.

I stare at Katie's disaster of an apartment; realizing that the chaotic placement of all these particles came from a catalog of tiny decisions, brief moments of near-intention. Euphoria floods my brain, brought on by a frenzy of solitude, and at this very instant I think I could die content. That's the signpost of pure bliss. That's when you know it can't get any better.

But it doesn't last. The moment you reach the top of the mountain, there's just so much ogling over the panorama before it's time to climb back down. Instead of dying I turn on some music and sit down on the couch among the congregation. Before long the song ignites my restless legs. I don't just want to sit around waiting for life to come to me. Should I walk to the door and open it? Nothing out there but the whole entire world. Nothing but footsteps and a million roads going everywhere. Confusion, headaches, heartaches mixed in. It's a symptom of freedom to be enslaved by the endlessness of possibility.

So I pick up a brush and dip it in the oil and I smear stupid purple lines on a piece of paper.

Life is governed by the hours, and the hours are governed by the sun. The sun is governed by immeasurable spaces between the tiny vibrations of matter. I should be so small, to look outward with longing eyes, so that everything I see becomes vast potentiality. But if I am the sum of my experiences, then I am also the clouds, the mountains, the television, slivers under the skin turning animals into cyborgs, reconstructing world from world, smushing putty under the thumb and then stretching again to plod through the leeward side of the tip of my tongue.

Fuck it. I'm going out.

CHAPTER THREE

THE OXFORD

Prescott, AZ

Years ago I fell for this gorgeous redhead while I was waiting in line at a grocery store. She stood ahead of me, digging for coupons. I thought to myself, *Sweet stardust, that's one sexy lady!*

A bored checkout clerk slid her groceries over the beeping glass. He would be the liaison for my seduction. I leaned across the conveyor belt and whispered like a tornado in a drainpipe, "Hey, do you see the woman over there? The one digging for coupons?"

My eyes darted suggestively femaleward. Yes, just like two little round darts.

"Uh," the clerk hesitated, wondering whether he should warn me about my volume control.

"That's right," I said. "The pretty one. The one you are currently ringing up. There is no other girl anywhere near us. I suppose you'll be giving her a receipt soon."

"Yeah," he intoned. Oh, did he intone.

"Do you think I've got a chance with her? I mean, do you think she'd ever go to dinner with me?"

"Hm," uttered the clerk. He needed to utter something cleverer than that. I was sinking here and I couldn't do this alone.

Then he said, "Well she mostly bought frozen dinners, so she may be hard up for a decent meal."

That's more like it.

"Good point," I said. "I'll have to take her somewhere nice. But she's a knockout. Just look at her. She probably has a boyfriend, huh?"

I could hear her chuckling into her purse.

Our clerk said, "Maybe. No wedding ring, though. And I don't get the feeling she's shopping for two." He was really starting to get into this.

"Well I'm going to go for it," I said. "Damn the torpedoes. Listen, I'm a little shy when it comes to talking with women. What do you say you let me write my phone number on the receipt before you hand it to her? Can you do that? Does it break any transaction laws?"

"I could lose my job," he said with all seriousness, scanning three coupons in succession.

"Maybe, but this could be the real thing. You don't want to spend the rest of your life wondering if you let something as silly as minimum wage get in the way of true love."

"You make a strong case." Our clerk rang up the total. I still remember that magic number, $27.44.

I waited in silence, fidgeting with my can of honey-roasted peanuts and a bag of carrots. I could have gone through the express lane that day, but for some reason I just didn't. It wasn't even the thought: who needs express lanes, or anything like that. I'd simply stepped into the regular lane and there she was.

She paid by check. The clerk glanced at her ID. "Thank you, Miss," he said coyly. Then he yawned, stretched, and with the sort of mock secrecy that is painfully obvious, tore her receipt from the register and handed it to me.

I scrawled down my name and number.

"I think there's been some mistake," I said, surreptitiously handing the receipt back to him. "This isn't mine."

"You're right," he said. "How stupid of me."

The clerk gave the receipt to the woman. She turned toward me and without a word offered me her grocery bags. I donned the cap of chivalry and carried them to her car, leaving my peanuts and carrots behind. She opened the passenger door and I set her bags on brown vinyl covered in white dog hair. "You have a dog?" I asked.

"He's an Airedale," she said.

I watched her put the receipt in her purse. Then there was a lot of coy glancing and awkward shifting of weight. She parted her lips and for some reason I thought she was about to start singing. "You should call me sometime," she said.

"Okay," I said. But I didn't have her number; she had mine. As she got in her car and drove away I decided it would not have been a horrible idea to point that out.

1.

My mind roars with the destinationless thrill of motion. Leaving my spatula and plush congregation behind, I make for the bridge. Once in sight, and close enough to hear the white roar of the river below, I am struck by a five-year-old's need to piss. I can hear my mother's voice in my head telling me I should've gone before I left the house. I don't really want to backtrack all the way to Katie's. Fortunately, there's an alley behind Flippers that'll do the trick.

I hobble back across the street, knees clenched, failing to perform even a remotely casual variation of the peepee-jog. It occurs to me that a man repressing his nature always looks a little like a jackass.

For the last few steps I give up all pretense and dash into the alley, where a flimsy blue dumpster slumps like a dead whale on the sand.

I shift back and forth. My thighs jiggle. If my zipper were a bra-clasp I would not have fumbled more. Finally free, I prop myself against the lid, cock in hand, and counting off the distance from my bladder to the ground, let loose those salty silver drops.

"I bet your first born I can limbo that there glistening fount and not get a drop on me."

Just beyond the arc of that glistening fount, standing like a cardboard cutout, the shadow of Katie's ex makes his wager. The very sound must have summoned him to the scene. A djinn of the gutter, a connoisseur of unmasked moments—the happy bard's ears have led him into the sort of grand entrance he's been waiting for all his life.

Standing there all Nordic and lopsided, Adam Jostler folds his arms, gazes at ground zero, and ponders its erosion. He stands at least seven inches taller than me, five more in his wide, green hat. A rosewood guitar slung across his back. Sparse sideburns trickle down his jaw. A gallant needlepoint mustache glides over his cheek-bones, stabbing the joints of his bristling blonde beard.

"You got a lot in you, buddy. Saving up for days. Saving for just this moment. It's how you are, Mister Wagner. What do you say—will you wager your progeny against the stability of your steaming parabola?"

Adam tips his hat and cracks his knuckles. I glance at him without a word. He sort of ducks his head like he's going to bend over. He pantomimes a slouch and says, "You don't mind if I—" And his next movement is merely a grin. Not only true to his word, but lilting now, innocent and cartoonish, and without even removing his hat, Adam crab-walks like a defective puppet to emerge dry as a bishop on the far side. Then up again a new man, facing the trash bin, arms outstretched for inspection.

"That's all she wrote! Say goodbye to the proudest pound of flesh that dangling participle could ever produce. You can visit on weekends. Look at you, still going strong! What eternal well of life do you drag around down there?"

I chuckle deep inside so my body bounces and the stream staggers into leaflets of pee. Then the smile passes. Piss at last diminished, becoming a dribble, folded away and zipped up. "I'm never having kids," I say.

"That's what Katie used to say." Adam's smile takes on a maudlin nostalgia. "Have you seen her? Katie, I mean."

"Yeah," I say.

"Is she okay?"

It breaks my heart not to tell him Katie's still a virgin, because it's clear he's worried about who the baby-daddy is and whether he even still has a chance with her at this point. They've been broken up a long time now, but who knows. They say a baby changes every-thing. I can't tell him there's no father, though, because I'm sworn to secrecy. Whether he thinks she cheated on him or not, it's pretty clear he's still in love with her. I'm sure Katie knows this. I think girls always know, even if sometimes they say they don't. It's all tactics.

"She hasn't been dating anyone," I tell him.

"Oh I know," he retreats. "It isn't that. I'm just curious how she's holding up."

"She seems fine. She's about due."

He nods carefully, backing away from the topic. Then he strangles both sides of his belly with his huge hands and gives it an accordion squeeze. He looks up and says to me, "What about breakfast?"

"What about it?"

"Someone makes it. We eat it," says he. "Let's go before I die. Got any money?"

For custom's sake I fish around in my pockets, but I already know the answer. Not even enough for toast. I continue to dig, fingers swirling the empty pouch like a turbine.

"It's okay," says Adam. "We've got friends all up and down Higgins. I know at least two people I can talk into owing me money."

2.

Missoula's population is small enough that everyone knows everyone, but it's large enough that there's not enough time for everyone you know. Missoula is right in the annoying middle, population-wise. Like the awkward teenager version of a city. Katie used to say, "You see so many people on the street that you kinda-sorta know—or maybe met once or twice at a show—that if you stopped to talk to them all you'd never make it to where you're going." Dealing with all this leads to the unspoken social convention of not acknowledging anyone until you know them *really* well. There have been times where I couldn't establish eye contact with the same person who told me their life story only a week before. On the other hand, I've found that a lot more people are willing to meet and have an honest conversation when they know they won't have to pay for it later with large chunks out of their schedule.

Adam has never worried about this sort of thing. He will meet you and be your friend if you want and that's all there is to it.

Adam's green overcoat sweeps his ankles. His spine is joyful and straight. A few years back he lost a canine and most of the tooth next to it when an SUV full of douchebags jumped him just for looking strange. This has no impact whatsoever on his ability to smile at almost anything that goes down. Adam is a career grinner. He smiles the way the rest of us breathe, and his smile is always genuine. It's a lot of hard work to smile that often with so much sincerity. Try it for a while and see if you have the energy left over to hold down a real job.

We walk back toward the bridge, but instead of crossing, Adam leads us down the slope and into the park where we stand side-by-side staring over the river's vagrant flow.

Without looking away from the water, he reaches into his pocket and produces a half-bitten shell, holds it out to me. "Peanut?"

"For breakfast?"

He tosses the peanut into the current. It bobs and floats away like a message in a bottle. "Let's swim," he says.

"They made that bridge for a reason," I say.

"A swim will wake you up."

"I've been awake for hours."

"I haven't," Adam argues. "Come on, it's warm. When's the last time you swam across the river?"

"Never. Isn't it seven years bad luck to swim before you eat?"

"That's after. Come on."

"What about your guitar?"

"Some hippie gave it to me. Let's just leave it here for the next guy."

3.

Dean always used to say that if cell phones had hit the market ten years earlier, Katie Ludwick and Adam Jostler would never have fallen in love.

The day they first met was shortly after Katie and Amelia decided to take a road trip around the U.S. in a gutted-out RC Cola van. The girls insulated their van with egg crates and installed bunk beds in the back. They read "On the Road" from the road, and lived the Kerouac dream. I caught the tail end of that trip on my way back home from India. We all met up in Pismo Beach. We wrapped Katie in seaweed and dragged her into the surf. We stole an American Flag. We drove a convertible the wrong way up the freeway ramp and fixed their van's broken stick shift with duct tape and spare pieces of home hardware. We got drunk and screamed at the sea and the stars and made them promise to keep up the good work. We spent an entire day in Wal-Mart taking pictures of items with a disposable camera snatched off the shelves. Then we dropped the camera off at the Wal-Mart development station. Two hours later we got the pictures back and placed each one next to their original subject. We left the store empty handed and debated whether what we'd done counted as stealing.

All the while their great American adventure was underway, they'd left their house in the care of another girl also named Katie. When they finally got back to Missoula, Amelia and Katie Ludwick took over the house again, and the other Katie found a place of her own. It just so happened that this other Katie and Adam Jostler were good friends at the time, and one day, shortly after the other Katie moved out and our Katie moved back in, Adam called the house looking for the other Katie. He called using his friend's black rotary wall phone. Katie's orange rotary wall phone rang and Amelia answered. Adam said, "Is Katie there?" and Amelia handed the phone to Katie Ludwick.

"It's Adam," Amelia said, thinking the call was for our Katie and not the other Katie. But our Katie had never met Adam Jostler. She did have a friend named Adam Nickerson, though, and she assumed it must be him on the line.

Because Katie was in a hurry that day, she and Adam made quick plans to meet up, each thinking the other was someone else. "Come down to Flippers in an hour. I'll be on the machines," Katie said, and hung up the phone.

When Adam arrived, Katie Ludwick was the only person in the casino. Adam was about fifteen minutes late, so he walked up to her and said, "I'm looking for my friend Katie. Has anyone else been in here in the last half hour?"

Katie Ludwick looked up into the glow of the keno machine reflecting off his wide, gentle eyes and fell instantly in love. Adam fell in love too, but for him it happened a few minutes later when, following an awkward exchange of confused questions, both of them realized how the whole mix-up had gone down. Epiphanies collided and he did swoon.

The new couple found an apartment and moved in together the very next month. Adam paid his friend ten bucks for the phone he'd used to make that fortuitous call, and packed it with his stuff. Katie brought along her orange phone, and they set them side-by-side on the table and never plugged either of them into the wall.

4.

In mid-winter, Missoula's Clark Fork River becomes a junkyard. Creeping west beneath the Higgins Bridge, she freezes into a slush mill of ice and jutting driftwood. Twists of metal piping, chicken wire, a fallen telephone pole, even an overturned couch upholstered in frost—everything dry-docked in this dwindling whisper between encroaching banks of snow.

In mid-summer she is a highwater railroad of revenge, pulling down trees, fence posts, and the occasional fisherman. Luckily by this time of year she's finally starting to chill out again. It's still warm enough that we probably won't catch hypothermia. I stare at the ghostly swirls and peel off my socks while Adam strips down to nothing but.

"What about when we get across?" I hold my right boot up by the heel.

He puts a foot in the water and crinkles up his nose. "Hm?"

"Our clothes."

"Oh." Adam folds his hands on top of his head. He faces me naked and deflating in the wind. His furry belly flops forward, thoughtful.

Adam dashes off and comes back a few minutes later with a large plastic grocery bag, into which he stuffs his clothes. As he stuffs he periodically glances my way as if giving a demonstration.

"Where'd you find that?"

"The trash behind Flippers. It's clean."

"We're going to get arrested," I say.

"Okay, clothes go in bag. Bag goes on top of head. Like this."

"Okay."

"And I attach it to my head with the belt."

I watch him attempt this. He cinches it down with a notch to spare. I take off my hoodie. Adam balances the load. Off comes my shirt and I note a drop in temperature. Adam clasps the belt buckle under his chin as I unlatch my own, dropping my drawers in public for the second time in fifteen minutes. The bag begins to slip. Adam puts a hand up to steady it, and with my jeans slopped down around my ankles, I wait to see what will happen.

Adam dips a timid toe into the water. Somehow he manages to stabilize the laundry sack and advance another notch on the belt. His beard struts out in front of the leather strap like a fan. I step out of my pants, and bundle all my clothes together as Adam kneels down, opening up his head to receive them. Everything fits but the hoodie. I'm sure that if I had my boxer's jacket this wouldn't be a problem.

"Wrap it around your head," Adam says.

"Like this?"

"Okay. Let's go."

"I changed my mind. Give me my clothes."

"Too late."

"I'm serious."

"Jump in! All at once."

Two splashes off the bank. Kids lean over the bridge dropping stones. Others fly by in coiled up hot rods and motorcycles, going as fast as they can in case the bridge ever decides to collapse. A trail meets the slope on the far shore, in the middle of Caras Park, where it bulges and relaxes into the spread of downtown.

We swim where we can, keeping our heads above water. The first few seconds are almost paralyzing, but we splash around and adjust to the cold. Some college kids float by on inner tubes. We try to keep swimming even in the shallows. It sucks to put feet down on the rocks of a river bottom, so we avoid it at all cost, sometimes crawling along on our hands instead. A few small islands block our path. Adam gets out and walks, but I swim around, refusing to leave the water until I can put my clothes back on. Halfway across I remember what Amelia said about breaking the river. I decide to try it with my fist. The splash recoils and gets me in the face, in the eye. Adam looks back and asks me what I'm doing. "Nevermind," I say. Five minutes later we're both shivering on the farther shore.

"Gimme my pants," I demand, standing with naked arms wrapped around a naked chest, watering the grass beneath me.

"Boots. Shirt. You had two socks, right?"

"I'm freezing."

"Come on, it's still summer," he says. "How greasy do you want breakfast?"

I wrap, buckle, zip, button, lace. Adam wipes himself down with his jeans. Some ways off a family of four takes a walk through the park. The little boy points, and I flap hands at Adam to quicken up.

He says, "If you want maximum grease, the Oxford's

our best bet. I have a hangover, so I vote maximum grease. What do you want to eat?"

"Toast."

"Greasy toast?"

I'm still flapping, looking over my shoulder for the cops. Adam sticks his hand down the throat of a sock and stretches cotton-webbed fingers to the sun. Makes a fist, pulls the insides out in one swift tug.

"Put your pants on first," I say.

"Love thy tootsies above all else. Think of what they do for you. Do you know the foot has more natural curves per square inch than any other part of the body? What could be more provocative than bare feet?"

Last of all, Adam buffs his beard. He shakes and wrings and brushes until dry. Satisfied, he slaps his legs.

"Okay?"

"Breakfast."

"Grease?"

"Toast."

LAS VEGAS, NV

"Thanks for being there when I need you," she used to say, "and for not being there when I don't need you."

We liked to sit on the grass under a fig tree by the pool on the roof in the glow of Las Vegas lights, wrapped in the smell of a campfire, leaning out over a skywalk, trying to come across as clever, sincere, trustworthy, mysterious, wanton, aloof, desperate, insatiable, cool, easy, injured, vibrant, independent, eternally devoted.

I carved our initials into some wood. This is actually something people do.

"Mr. Wagner," she said, "—are you in love with me?"

"I'm under love with you," I said. I didn't want to give away the game. "Just barely below the love line, the demarcation between love and not-quite-love. I'm right under that."

"So watch my step is what you're saying."

When I pulled her toward me she fit perfectly in the awkward jutting curve-free jabby rib cage part of my right flank.

Sometimes I scared her. I lost my shit, tore out my hair, punched a wall, smashed a violin, panicked and trembled like a baby, grew distant, climbed out of bed at 3am to walk through still-sweltering streets, contemplated suicide, withdrew, refused to say what I was thinking.

"Yoshie, let's live on a sailboat."

We liked to go people watching. In malls, bars, casinos, theaters. Tried going to a theater to watch the audience instead of the show. Train stations were her favorite. Reunions and good-byes. "How many are falling in love, or thinking about divorce, lying to each other, pregnant and don't know it yet, developing cancer, hours from a car wreck..."

At home I dodged the heat by lying on the living room floor, eyes closed. Sometimes she'd crawl over and sing to me. Inches from my ear. Some raspy blues melody that made me hallucinate black-and-white images. Dark clouds with white glowing edges. Fields of grey grass. A silver carafe, empty. Vegas in the 20s. A high peak and a distant gulf that grew ever wider and rushed toward me at the same time.

"About the sailboat," she said, "I changed my mind."

This is actually something people do.

5.

Adam and I make our way out of the park, where brass sculptures of fish perch on grassy tumors, and the trail becomes a stone wall that vanishes into the brush and topples toward the river. At the heart of the park a great pavilion waits for concerts, festivals, impromptu pagan holidays, and farmers' markets—along with drug deals, games of human chess, and the occasional street musician.

"I have to stop here," Adam says, stopping in front of a white brick apartment building.

"What for?"

"I have to go in," Adam folds his hands behind his back and hops up and down like he's trying to see through one of the high windows. "Wait here."

"Okay."

"I'll just be a minute."

The door to the lobby flops back and forth and I'm alone with my thoughts. I gaze down the sidewalk toward the place where the bridge crests its own horizon. A bicycle rolls by. When it sinks beyond the summit I wiggle my fingers and say, "Zozezaz!" A small cloud swims behind the Wilma Theater and is gone. "Zozezaz," I incant. Predictable paths lead toward vanishing points. I feel better pretending to control them all. A bird flies under the bridge, "Zozezaz," and never re-emerges. Everything on its way out. What would be the last thing to go among the dregs of a dissolving world? And would that last thing be able to follow, surrounded by nothing at all, with nowhere even left to vanish to?

In much the same way, Vegas girl curled up and disappeared from my life. But there was this one moment, long before the end, when I could see it coming, when I knew she was going to leave me.

We were lying in bed. "I want ice cream, Yoshie," she said. I got up and drove her little red car down to the grocery store wearing only a bathrobe. A comfy purple bathrobe. Nothing underneath.

If it had been a book or a movie, a cop would have pulled me over, but that didn't happen. I drove carefully.

I imagined getting mugged on my way across the parking lot, ripping open the robe to flash the bastard and send him screaming into the wild Las Vegas streets.

I wanted something dramatic to happen so I could write a story about it. The night was hot. But it was just another moment in a wide net of moments. I guess I'd reached the age where I could walk out into the world naked but for a bathrobe and nothing weird was going to happen to me.

I picked up the ice cream and brought it back and she slurped it down with no expression. The light of the TV reflected in her unblinking eyes, and I realized how much better it is to want something than to get it. Longing is life. Possession binds you to the ground. I watched the ice cream melt all the desire out of her sweet face and I knew right then that we couldn't last. But for about thirty seconds it didn't really matter. For that one brief window in time she could have turned to me, touched my hand, told me it was over and that she was leaving forever, and it wouldn't have hurt at all.

By the time things really ended I couldn't think that way anymore. There are minutes, holes in the continuum, when disappointment can be the best thing in the world. And then that perspective rushes away and men become fragile as kindling once more.

Adam meets me back on the sidewalk. He snaps a dollar bill in front of my face. "Have you seen this man?"

"How much did you get?"

"Maybe three dollars. Coffee, toast and a side of grease. I want hash browns, too."

"We don't have enough."

"Swim felt good, don't you think?" Adam takes off his shirt again, balls it up and dries his armpits. He puts his thumbs up to his breast as if seeking suspenders to snap. He leans back on his heels and laughs. "Come on. A king's table awaits us at the Oxford."

6.

The Oxford all-in-one diner/bar/casino provides the autonomic metronome for Missoula's oldtown strip. Oldtown, though it isn't all that old, maintains legendary status as the historical heart of the city. The Ox started out in 1883 as a small grill in a teepee down by the Clark Fork river. In the 50s the Oxford moved to Broadway and then to its final resting place—the corner of Higgins and Pine.

Photographs, postcards, and portraits hang crooked along the Oxford's walls, telling Missoula's story in black and white—smudged and water-damaged with curled corners and insignificant signatures. Past patrons, old bartenders and cooks, hobos, good American pioneers, hard workers (or at least hard at work avoiding work), and the wrinkled mugs of old men from heavy north-western railroad—all of them old, foundational, regulars in their way. Frame after frame of tilted heads, squinted eyes, layers of skin like peaks and troughs in the stock market. What souls made highways and canyons of those wrinkles?

At the Ox you pay before they feed you. Once we're settled up our waitress brings out toast and hash browns and gravy and coffee and apple juice floating on one gigantic platter. I start in on the toast, scraping grape jelly waves against the crust. Adam doesn't touch his food. Says he wants to let the grease settle. He pulls out a pack of rolling papers, slips one loose and holds it out like he's offering a tissue.

"You want one?"

"I quit."

"Me too." Adam places a pinch of fresh tobacco in the middle of the paper and flattens it down with his fingertip.

I watch Adam rub the two sides of the rollie together in an up and down motion. Then he licks one edge. He does this by keeping his tongue in place and sliding the paper across it with both hands, right to left like a platen cylinder. Seals it into a marginally cone-shaped stub, and tucks it behind his ear.

"You quit, too, huh?" I leer with suspicion.

"Yep. This is just in case."

"In case you start again?"

Adam shoves a spoon into his breakfast. "I'm addicted to rolling them."

"There's no Tabasco sauce."

"I made a deal with the Devil," he says. "I am dying from the cancers, I told him. Help me quit smoking and I'll do anything, I told him. Do you know what the Devil said?" Adam hands a bottle my way.

"This is green."

"You've never had green Tabasco?"

"Seriously?"

"I used to take shots of this stuff. Try it. It's good. Anyway the Devil tells me he will cure my addiction, but there must be a trade! For Satan does not have the power to create or destroy, but only to sift."

"Sift?"

"Only to sift," he says. "No longer would I crave the smoke in my lungs, but from then on I'd be addicted to the act of rolling cigarettes. And so it goes. Conservation of addiction. One way or another I'm still hooked."

I rub my eyes, remembering my love for the Oxford like the secret blissful terror of psychedelics and roller coasters. That common thread of familiar suspicion and permissive creepiness evolving through any series of myth, madness, and in fact nostalgia—each of which has forever had a hand in seasoning Oxford evenings. Brains and eggs still on the menu and all is right with the world. It's the unabashed gutteresquity that draws us here. No deceit in the Oxford, no double-faced pleasantry. Everyone from bankers to preachers to millwrights to students to senators can be at their comfortable wormiest. Outrageous behavior might breed a delicacy of violence, but no one ever got a knife in the back, not yet anyway. Curses, insults, and respectful fist fights weave a counterintuitive grid of relative security over those who pass through the Oxford's jingling door.

Adam says, "So about Katie," as I shovel up a mouthful of hashed browns dripping green. "I haven't seen her since she kicked me out."

"That's pretty weird for this town," I say.

"Should I talk to her?"

"Do you want to talk to her?"

He stares me in the eye and the stare says: *She cheated on me, Josh.* But my counter-stare says, *No she didn't, you dumbass.* He doesn't catch on. He probably thinks my eyes are saying, *Yes, you're quite the chump, aren't you?*

Adam grabs a piece of toast and holds it out in front of his face. He looks more like a little boy than I've ever seen him, "Can I tell you something?"

"Sure."

"I haven't told anyone this, and it's starting to drive me crazy. I think I can trust you with the secret."

"Okay."

"I want her back," he says.

"That's a secret?"

There are these tiny, succulent moments when I can render Adam speechless that I wouldn't trade for anything.

"Everybody knows," I continue, "I'm pretty sure even Katie knows."

"That obvious?"

"Look," I tell him. "She hasn't dated anyone since you guys broke up. Why not tell her how you feel? Go nuts."

"I don't know."

"It's what you're supposed to do," I say.

"Maybe I should wait. Until after she has the baby."

"Just tell her. If she wants you back why wait any longer?"

His eyes go wide. "What if she doesn't want me back?"

"Then get rejected already so you can stop worrying about it."

"You think she'll reject me?" Adam says around a spoonful of grease.

"It is impossible to predict anything when it comes to women. It's all darts and blindfolds."

7.

But Adam no longer pays attention to me. Howls rise from the other side of the room. Chairs hit the floor. Five guys in a horseshoe formation stumble in. Five guys with single note of laughter passed between them, resonating throughout the chamber of their conjoined bodies.

Adam raises an eyebrow and glances over my shoulder acknowledging the sound. He gestures to me, indicating something I can't decipher. One of the five spots us. He's a heavy, lumbering guy whose baby face kind of floats out ahead of the onslaught. He points, directing his laughter our way, focusing it through a pair of lip rings.

"Hey!"

"Hey!"

"Hey!"

"Hey!"

Which is all still laughter, trying to take on the form of language—as if laughter itself were not language.

Adam recognizes them. He smacks out their names through dribbling gravy and I can't understand a word.

The guy who pointed rubs his bowling ball head with a deck of meaty fingers. "Adam has a cigarette," he shouts.

Oh?

The five seem to leap the length of the Oxford floor. They surround Adam, tackling him, groping toward him all at once. Adam dodges, presents the palm of his hand just in time to catch a face. Teeth gnash and a playful growl rises up as they tear at him like a pack of plush dogs.

Which is all still laughter, trying to take on the form of violence—as if laughter itself were not violence.

"Okay, okay! Just ask, okay? Ow!"

The skinniest of the five, long sandy hair knotted up, glasses twisted, teeth frozen against Adam's shoulder, without moving his jaw seems to say—*Can I have?*

The cigarette, dislodged from behind Adam's ear and now held tightly in his fist, is revealed slowly, inducing a mock gasp of surprise from the five. Somehow the cigarette survives the attack unharmed. Not so Adam's hair, which he pampers before setting on the task of four new rolls.

"I need more room!"

The five lead Adam to the last open table in the joint. They perch around his left shoulder as he hunches over his work.

But I'm not completely abandoned. Another man, a tagalong to the five in his late fifties, somehow ends up with the original cigarette. He lights it and falls into the chair across from me. He scratches an ear and tugs his short, grey beard.

"What was I saying?" he asks.

"Nothing," I tell him.

"Oh." He crosses his arms and leans forward to gaze into a cup of water. He savors his smoke and exhales against the plastic. Words follow, emerging from a fog, spilling across the table. Over the rim of his glasses peer tiny eyes, like those of a bird. They lock on mine. I have never before felt so much like I was part of a telepathic conversation.

The old man mutters, "I remember I was dreaming. And I remember knowing I was dreaming. And it was raining, or it had been. In the dream it was just after a rain. I was looking at my glasses, holding them up. There were little flat drops all over the lenses. And I remember one drop making a slow, jagged trail downward. I was looking at it, and now I can't seem to remember if it was on the outside or the inside of the lens. I kept thinking how amazing it was that I was dreaming and looking at it, and that I knew I was dreaming—my brain able to create this kind of detail. For itself. Able to create it and look at it and be amazed by it all at once."

Behind the man, the Oxford's back door opens, letting in a puff of wind. I can see the rectangle of daylight wrap around the head of my new companion, pushing all the leftover darkness inward and onto his face.

"What was I saying?"

I set my toast down, pick it up again and nibble the crust. "You were dreaming," For a second it seems like the man in front of me is a rubber toy, and that I should be squeezing him.

"Rain," I amend, tucking my hands under my thighs.

"Rain," the man repeats, drawing the word out and burying it in a cloud of smoke.

From the other table Adam coughs, then snorts. One of the five gives him a nudge. Four of them stand in a row opposite him, leaning against a single chair. The fifth, in torn jeans and long black jacket, with two red razor stripes racing down his neck, crouches beside Adam at the end of the table, locked in the tunnel of his sideburns. Adam hands him a cigarette without missing a beat.

8.

Over by the back door a man in a Cubs cap and white jacket has just entered the Oxford. He has sort of a doughy face and bright blue eyes intent on their work. There's a name tag on his jacket, but I can't read it. He leans down and picks up two crates, then turns back toward the door, waddling with a crate under each arm.

A waitress rushes toward him. Head waitress from the look of it. She wears a black hair net. Her face is painted on. Her fingers stab outward like iron webbing. "Excuse me! Excuse me!" She's spitting on the man, on purpose or not, all just coming out with her words.

The man turns to face her and says, "Listen. Listen. Listen," which is exactly what she refuses to do. The man bobs the crates up and down, a failed attempt at hypnosis.

The waitress' spine is bent in at least five places. Her bones must be wires. Her skin sags in folds and pouches. She continues spitting. "You can't take those. No. You cannot take those. Who do you think you are?"

"This is my job, lady. You want to see the paperwork?"

The man sitting across from me says, "A raindrop crawling down the lens, leaving streaks like frozen lightning."

"Who the hell do you think you are?" shrieks the

waitress. "Put those crates down right now, goddammit or I'll have you hauled away."

"Look. Look at the paper, lady."

"Have *you* hauled away."

"Look at the words." The man clutches the crates and holds out a pink receipt.

Her hands go straight to her hips—eyes nowhere near his papers. Curses tangle like marbles in her lips.

She's trembling, and her face bears defeat. Other waitresses inch near, hesitating, glancing at each other for guidance.

"You don't open this door. Not without knocking." She's no longer screaming. Retired words reduced to a choked futility. "You don't take these crates. You can take your paperwork right back to your boss and have him shove it up his hole."

Most of the customers remains in their own isolated worlds. At one point I see a single glance shoot back, but no one else really takes much notice. I've never felt so disjointed, so disconnected with everything. There was a time when the world made sense, when it felt like a cohesive unit. Now there are only splinters and fragments.

I look at Adam, still huddled in mid-roll, and now his shoulders seem to be rowing. The five suck down their cigarettes, pantomiming a riot, their eyes glowing bright for the duration of each drag, cheeks pulled tight. But only the man in front of me exhales. Exhaling the smoke that the others take in.

The crate man says, "It's just my job, okay? Like you have a job, I have a job. I have to take these—listen, calm down. I have to take these crates. I have to—"

The old man tells me: "The background in a mist. I remember thinking it was Japan in the early morning."

I've already forgotten what he was trying to say.

"I was too focused on the drop," he says. "I couldn't see the background. It was blurred past my perception, like an oil painting, water-damaged, curled up and bending over my back."

"The raindrop?"

"The world."

Adam is tossing cigarettes now—one, two, three, four—into the open mouths of his patrons, who swallow them whole and beg for more. I can hear Adam pinching and licking and handing over. The five smoke faster than he can roll. The conversation long faded away. No time for it. Dive straight for the source. Their addictions play off one another into a perpetual fever derailed from the track of time. A man shoveling dirt into the air.

Somewhere between desire and contentment there are tiny fractures, cracks of panic. Moments where continuity is lost and reason cannot find it again. Isolated space dissected from the thread of reality, where passion emerges spontaneously, and something is free to arise from nothing.

"Get out of my bar." The waitress is nearly in tears.

The man in the white coat doesn't move. "I have papers. Papers say that I can take these."

"Never come back. Never come back here."

The crate man turns away. He's about the closest he'll ever get to permission. But at the last instant the waitress shudders, twists and flails her arms as if she were breaking loose of her own elbows. With a groan she tears at him with hands and nails and spit, knocking one of the crates out from under his arm.

The crate splinters on the ground. Conversations pause, skipping like a scratch on a record, then, realizing all the fuss is only a crate, continue.

I see myself broken into wooden bits, lying on the kitchen floors of a dozen diners across America.

I feel like an alien. I've returned to Missoula, but am I really home?

When I stand up the man across from me doesn't seem to notice. He stares at my belt and says, "The drop reflected everything, just like a real drop. Such detail. Such precision. Such clarity of thought."

Chips of wood. The waitress sobbing. Her face open flat like a ledger on a pedestal of hands.

I need to get out of here, I think, though not in so many words.

The man in the white coat hustles out the back door, trying to appear as if he's just passing on through. One crate remains under his arm.

I spare a glance to see if Adam is still rolling. His shoulders whir like a hummingbird. A cloud of smoke hovers over their table like a thunderhead—heavy, ready to burst into rain at any moment, extinguishing its source.

A young waitress comes out from behind the bar with a broom in one hand, creeping up on the pile of splinters.

As I reach for the door it opens ahead of me. To my surprise, Amelia is standing there as if wrapped in a bow.

"Mister Wagner," she laughs. And then she really laughs, doubling over.

What's so funny?

"Come out here with me at once!"

CHAPTER FOUR

BROKEN

Denver, CO

My record for breakups with one woman is nineteen. She was a beautiful Chippewa princess with licorice hair and a kiss so soft you only felt it as a lump in your throat. We first met in New Orleans, and then randomly in San Francisco, but mostly we hung out in Denver. We'd breakup and get back together again like a circadian rhythm. She was better at the breaking up part, instigating thirteen of them, while I can only take credit for five. The getting back together part was more-or-less down the middle. Our fifteenth breakup was the most painful. The eighth one was pretty hilarious, looking back. Breakups four and five could probably be considered two sides of the same breakup, and there's still some debate over that, but I'm sticking with calling them two separate breakups. Breakup number one was just stupid and neither of us really understood why it went down. I remember breakup eighteen like staring out over a red canyon with high tide rising at my back. I have no memory of breakup nineteen; I just know it must've happened.

Sometimes it takes nineteen breakups to do the trick. Sometimes a thing has to be broken over and over again before it can be fixed for good.

Some love goes away. Some love never goes away. You have to go away from love before you can find out if love ever plans on going away from you. But if you stray too far then lingering love can become a haunting thing. It influences every dream. It hides under the finger-nails of every decision. You may have gone away from it, but it stays with you, clinging to your shoulders, and the road back feels a hundred times longer. It becomes burdensome, not because of the love, but because of the road. The road presses up on the feet of the traveler haunted by love.

There are exes you can see again, go out drinking with, flirt and laugh with. There are exes you can meet on a lonely evening for a fuck and a smoke. And there are exes with whom it is too dangerous to allow even a moment's eye contact. These are not exes at all, and never will be, and that's the problem.

1.

Once again on Amelia's arm, I am pulled back toward the fulcrum of the bridge. We sway as we walk, and Amelia's sprightly mannerisms slowly untangle the strange mood left by my experience in the Oxford.

Amelia asks, "What did you do today?"

"I hate that question," I say.

"Don't be a prick. Just tell me."

"Aren't we a little past small-talk?"

Amelia cracks the knuckles in her left hand. "Boys are very stupid. Small talk is the overture to big talk. You can't just dive directly into a deep conversation."

"Why not?"

"Because everything needs a reference. Everything evolves from a simpler entity. From something small and trivial. Trees grow from seeds. Chickens from eggs. Meaning must develop over time."

"This conversation got deep pretty fast."

"Yes, that is because you and I are well practiced. But it wouldn't have happened at all if I hadn't asked about your day."

We head west as the sun kneels on the horizon. The river flows in our direction under a canopy of wires sprouting from two lanes of splintering old telephone poles. When we've all upgraded to smartphones and brain implants, will this legacy of giants remain? There must be millions of them in the United States alone, clustered in neighborhoods and stretched out across the plains like totems of information.

Amelia says, "How was the Oxford?"

"A waitress freaked out about some crates."

"Typical." She pauses to straighten her tights.

"Adam was there."

"Oh yes? How is he?"

"Brokenhearted."

"He loves her," she says.

"He'd make a great dad if he could get his shit together."

Amelia nods. "And probably even if he can't."

"Maybe he really is the father."

"There is no father," she says.

"You believe that?"

"When was the last time Katie lied about anything?"

She has me there. I can do nothing but change the subject. I ask, "And how many boys are pining over you these days?"

"A few," Amelia's rubs her hands together like a mad-scientist. "My dating habits resemble solar systems. There is always one guy who is the sun, and then there are the planets, and occasionally I flirt with satellites. Every now and then I make out with an asteroid belt. But if I were to commit and only date the sun, I would become bored and wander away. The poor men I date for no other reason than to keep some other man at the precise distance where dating him remains possible."

A woman as complex as Amelia requires high-level mathematical formulas to maneuver her relationships.

"The real question is, who's been breaking your heart,

Mister Wagner?"

"We break our own hearts," I say.

"Oh?"

"Love is the universe striking two stones together over and over until there's a spark. It isn't something anyone does. Who is qualified to judge it? How can there be any real blame in there anywhere?"

Amelia thinks it over, not quite following. "Hmmm."

"Okay, it's like this. You and I are friends. I could go weeks without calling you and it wouldn't make a difference. But when love steps in, even a couple days of silence can cause a dent. If we're friends and I stand you up for a date it might be annoying, but if we're in love and I stand you up, it's devastating."

"Same behavior. Two effects."

"Right. So instead of saying so-and-so broke my heart, it should be: I have broken my heart against you."

She tries out the phrase, "I broke my heart against your heart." Suddenly she takes my arm. "Come on."

"Where are we going?" I ask.

"To gather the masses," she says.

2.

Amelia and I bounce about Higgins, weaving a drunken saw-tooth through Missoula until dusk. Along the way we absorb stragglers, one or two at a time until our gang resembles a class of grade-schoolers on a field trip. We run into Freedom and Megan skipping down the sidewalk; Jake, Slink, and Beatrice around the corner from Missoula's giant Bill the Cat statue; Margie and Jan and Barb and Paul bounce out of a casino. By the time our ranks surpass a dozen Amelia springs her plan.

"There's a party at Katie's house," she says.

"Does Katie know about this?"

"Certainly not."

"When does it start?"

"As soon as we arrive."

What a fisher of men is Amelia Tigerheart.

More! We need more humans. It becomes a game to see how many we can gather. We are the Great Attractor, a multiplying, morphing mob of merriment.

Butterfly Herbs is our first filling station. Tucked into the main strip of downtown, Butterfly is an apothecary, a coffee shop, a deli, and the sipping, sniping, doodling, riotous center of Missoula's renegade arts community. Everyone who works at Butterfly Herbs doubles as a regular. It's hard to tell when someone is on the clock or not. Baristas flow from countertop collaborations to booth-side hugs to the back alley for a smoke, while customers often hop up to get their own coffee, or go back to the cooler for more cream.

They're all artists or writers or musicians or aspiring filmmakers or old rainbow festival shaman-types or young hitchhiking tribal punks with bright green eyes and crooked yellow teeth, wrapped in hand-stitched puzzles of patch, earth tones, rainbows, scarves, buttons, tatters and thread. The backs of most of their hands smudged in black or red stamps from the night before. In Missoula everyone knows everyone, but in Butterfly, everyone knows everyone's story. A basketful of peers, friends, and lovers, the blazing youth of the northwest, unconcerned and unaware of how quickly they are rushing into the future. Spirits of the earth. In Butterfly they gather for inspiration, conversation, caffeine, and mutual hangover recovery sessions.

Everyone not absorbed in a masterpiece turns to look at us. I soak in the sight—these emerging Missoulians who dress up like gypsies, drink like rock stars, converse like debutante savants, cuss like rednecks, fight like assholes, and love like hippies. I am in awe of each and every one of them.

Alice, wearing a coat made entirely out of neckties, raises her hand like a first grader with a fierce need for recess. Her eyebrows bounce over blue horn-rimmed gramma glasses, and her grin bursts at its edges. "I will call some people who know people and they'll tell some bands who know bands to come and play," she shouts.

Beside her, Mark, ever snug in Double Windsor, vest, and patchwork pants, combs through his wiry Rasputin beard. His mascara wears thin. His head crests the top of my shoulder. Mark can reference Sam Keith, Dorothy Parker, and Georges Bataille in the same sentence with no accident of accuracy. "How do you always look so sharp?" I ask him.

"Victorian England is my guide. Men have forgotten how to dress. Cuff links," he points to his wrists, "for instance."

Len, sitting across from him, chuckles softly. Always composed, Len is the proud owner of the most Cheshire grin I have ever seen—and I've seen a few. He will pause for a brief second of thought before speaking, and when he speaks, he speaks in aphorism. Like it's his job to run around tying up conversations. On one side of Len sits Carissa, perpetually fourteen, incorruptible sprite; and on the other is Jayne, voracious gobbler of drugs and juggler of beats. She plays chess with Watson, an artist of quiet composition who is 99% satyr, 1% stone.

Back out on Higgins our pilgrimage nears thirty souls. The hours have fled and the mountains have slurped up the sun. We meander into the Wilma, the Howards, then down East Front Street, stopping now and again to get high—a different kind of high at every home. No one is ever quite ready to go when we arrive. We become a great pestering thing, an amorphous orrery, tethered by the precision of inside-jokes. Be thou assimilated! Share our flasks and tobacco. Interlocking arms, elbows hugflung neck to chin, passing one another from shoulder to shoulder, we invade living rooms, spill onto back porches, and scale rooftops.

We are pawns to the vibrations of stars, united until we arrive at our final destination. Then, with a drop of dish soap, our cabal is fractured. We split into triplets and couplets, some on their own, running to merge with friends who have preceded us, and eventually surging through Katie Ludwick's front door, our clan of forty-nine.

3.

Katie is not yet home to witness the flood. Some of us pounce upon the stereo, others begin to cook. Her fridge is emptied to make room for beer.

Amelia swings her arms wide and spins around. "I'm going to dance. But first, I'm going to smoke."

We linger on the porch. I slump down in the ripped out backseat of an 80s van. Amelia perches in an orange vintage barber's chair. It's old. Real old. Old enough to have chrome ashtrays in the arm rests. The porch is trimmed with kettles and woks, with sleeping bags, hammocks, and bicycle tires.

Amelia exhales a curtain of smoke, and as it parts she says, "So tell me more about this girl."

"Vegas girl?"

"Unless there's another one."

"What's to tell? We broke up."

Her whole countenance drops when I say this. "You did?"

"Yeah, kind of."

"Kind of a little bit?"

I think it over for a second, but it's just the wishful kind. "No. Kind of entirely."

Amelia investigates my eyes. "So. She's down there and you're up here, and you're pretty sure it's over but you aren't exactly ready for it to be."

"Something like that."

Her fingers touch the hem of my shirt and she says, "I'm going to tell you a secret. Are you ready?"

"What secret?"

"You're happy."

I snort with cynicism. "Uh, no. I'm fucking miserable."

"Did she cheat on you? Did she tell you she needs 'space'?"

"I can't even begin to describe it."

She touches my arm. "See, that's love. You're happy. You just don't know it. You probably won't know it until it's too late, but right now—this moment—this is the happiest moment of your life. And if you're very lucky, you'll realize it for a split second and that split second will get burned into your brain and you'll remember it later on when everything really is shit, and the memory will be what it takes to keep you going." She looks away. "I guess that's the tragedy."

"I don't think so," I argue. "I've been happy before, I know what it feels like, and it doesn't feel like this."

"You have no idea what happiness feels like," Amelia says. "You remember some sort of chemical-overload from the moments when everything was going your happy-go-lucky way. Remember? Tra-la-la! Birds and meadows. But that was not happiness. That was a trance you lived through. That was electroshock therapy. This? This right here—holding your guts in your hand—this is happiness."

"Well, then happiness sucks."

"But it's still happiness, and it still does what it's supposed to do. Do you want her back?"

I shrug. "Most of me does."

Amelia regains her drill-sergeant posture. "Then you must go back down there and apologize at once."

"Apologize?"

"That's right."

"Um..."

She leans forward in the barber chair and wags a finger in my face. "Don't try to figure out who's to blame. When you're done expressing your anger—which is what I suppose coming back to Montana was all about—your next move is to apologize. Immediately."

"That's unfair."

"That's love."

"Is this like your small-talk thing?"

"Yes. There are lots of rituals involved when it comes to women. And there are dance steps, and there is body language, and none of it has to do with anything, but it is all there to facilitate the passage of time. The passage of time is key."

"I think I give up."

"That's a good start. Let's go. I hear music." She smashes her cigarette into the protruding half-moon ashtray on the barber chair armrest and throws herself to the floor.

4.

A band plays homemade instruments in Katie Ludwick's back yard beside a fire pit of blackened stones. Tonight the kids dress like their grandparents. Accordions and banjos cling to threadbare suspenders. Pink octagon glasses and civil war caps. Flannel scarves and Balkan mustaches. We're just babies in thick glasses, plain cotton dresses, aprons, and a slight curl to our hair. Reincarnations of distant ancestors, our inheritance stolen from second hand stores.

I close my eyes to the accordion drone as the firelight flickers like a crime scene. I indulge in the desperation of trying to catch this moment in words, but the holes in my language-net are gaping and a moment is so very small.

A goat walks by. Two little horns. Grey beard. Chewing on something. This almost surprises me. "What's with the goat?" I ask.

"It's a party goat," someone says. "It loves beer."

"Whose is it?"

"Dunno. I think it's a rental."

Amelia and I dance for a while, but I soon get bored and go inside to see if Katie's back. We're all dying to see how she reacts to the shindig. We'll call it a baby shower if we must.

"Ahoy, varmint!" Dean cries from within. His voice is loud, plush, and belligerent, slowing down all other sound in the room. Adam stands beside him, grinning the grin of the great grey goose. Occasionally I see his eyes scan the room for some sign of Katie Ludwick.

"She's not here yet," I tell him.

"Come drink of the whiskey!" Dean leaps across the room in three lumbering steps. He seems happy, energized. In moments like these I forget how tenuous his grip on reality can be, how a shift in the breeze can elevate some delusion to overpowering strength. I am glad he's here, focused on the moment and not brooding over his ex-wife or the innumerable conspiracies that even now lie dormant in his subconscious.

"Where's Will?" I ask.

"Developing some sort of neural network or something on his computer," Dean says.

We are bloodhounds moving through the kitchen. Adam digs beer bottles from molehills of ice.

"You forgot the jacket again," I say, scowling.

"What jacket?" Dean mumbles.

"The blue boxers jacket you gave me. I need it."

"You don't need it."

"I want it."

"Well why didn't you say so?"

"I did!"

"I haven't seen that jacket in months. I think Katie has it."

SEATTLE, WA

Ages back, when I was watching a friend's house for a few months in Seattle, I got stuck inside a woman. Yes, by that I mean exactly what you think I mean. Stuck. Inside her. She apparently suffered from some sort of medical condition and this relentless contraction was a rare reaction. We stopped and kind of stared at each other. She blushed. I didn't move. I offered a quizzical glance in lieu of having the wherewithal to say anything whatsoever. "This has happened before," she said. "It could last for up to an hour, but in a minute you'll, you know, shrink down, and everything will be fine." But I didn't and it wasn't. The pressure, and perhaps the novelty, actually turned me on more. I expanded; she contracted.

"Just think about baseball or something," she said, annoyed. After an awkward moment she slapped me in the face. I guess she hoped the shock would wither me. Again, opposite effect. It all reminded me of something a friend once told me about dating girls with small hands. I thought if this went on I might end up prying her apart—work her down, break her resolve.

"We could be here for a while," she said.

There are these giant beetles in South Africa who crush empty beer cans. When they come across a discarded can of bud light in the desert they grab it in their pincers—pincers as long as their abdomens—they grab it and they crush it. Sometimes they crush it twenty or twenty-five times over. They're dusting their pincers with flecks of aluminum. Then they go and show female beetles how shiny their pincers are and the females go all weak in the knees for that shit.

The Ceratoid anglerfish is a deep-sea monster with goblin jaws and teeth like icicles. This fish has to win some galactic award for the number one screwball mating practice. It goes down like this:

Female anglers grow to over five feet long, but the males are only about the size of your fist. The males smell their way over to the females. When a boy angler finds a lady angler, he takes his baby goblin jaws and bites down on her ass. He doesn't let go, first because his saliva fuses his lips to her skin, but more importantly because as soon as a male anglerfish is born his digestive system breaks down and he starts to disintegrate. The only way the male anglerfish can stay alive is by feeding off a female, grabbing onto some girl fish and never letting go.

So now this crazed anglerfish, literally love-starved, dangles off his girlfriend's booty like a dead pit bull. He becomes a parasite. An extension of her circulatory system. He sucks nutrients from her body while she swims around minding her own business. But it's not enough, because even though he's slowed down the process, the male's body still continues to dissolve. His eyes drop out of his head. He atrophies and falls to pieces until there's nothing left but a pair of fish balls that finally, in one last gasp, explode into a cloud of sperm that fertilizes the female's eggs.

Then there are those little jumping spiders that look

like they're teleporting everywhere. Once a year the mandibles of all the males swell up so they can't eat. The go crazy with hunger, and they all start thronging together into this big mosh-pit of death, killing the fuck out of each other. They do this on top of the females. Hundreds of them. In their death throes they unload all over the ladies, setting the stage for the next battle royale.

A significant percentage of animal sperm cells are useless for fertilization. These aggressive sperms accompany the creative sperms like bodyguards— assassins that hunt down and kill the sperm of competing males.

Fig wasps go at it before they're even born. Mating is the first rite of passage to existence. If you don't mate, you don't get to live.

Banana slugs are hermaphrodites who devour each others' penises in the name of love.

Some lady ducks have labyrinthine vaginas, and male earwigs carry a backup cock.

The next time I saw Seattle girl was a couple years later. She'd had a kid, but she was single. I remember wondering if she'd trapped any other guys since me, any more relationships where she had trouble letting go. I think I would have been jealous to find out. It didn't bother me at all to think of her with other men, only to picture her giving anyone else that bashful gaze and clinical apology. Or slapping them in the face.

I had to wonder if her condition had any effect on the delivery of her child. Did he have to fight his way out?

Among sea horses it's the males who carry and bear the young.

Most reef fish females will take a turn being male at some point in their life.

Of all the bizarre accounts of parthenogenesis, including the case of Katie Ludwick, the weirdest by far occurs all the time in the insect world. The culprit of this condition is not genetic, but bacterial. The Wolbachia pipientis is a bacterium that lives in the sex organs of around 15% of all insect species. Since the Wolbachia can only be transmitted from host mother to host child, these bacteria have adopted strategies for limiting the number of pesky male offspring, who are useless to their cause. In certain cases, like mad alchemists, the Wolbachia mess with the insects' hormones and actually change their male hosts into females. In other cases the bacteria stops productive mating or eliminates the males of a population altogether, and parthenogenesis takes over as a last resort in maintaining the species.

Virgin pregnancy is nature's Hail Mary.

As a species we understood this long before science confirmed the reality. From folktales and footnotes to Hellenic festival, and finally a cornerstone of the western church, the ripened virgin represents hope both for the empty who long to be fulfilled, as well as for the overfull, tormented by a desire for purgation.

And a child conceived spontaneously—such as Katie Ludwick's—occurs to us as both stillborn and immortal.

5.

The hours pale by. This is the darkest before the dawn. Eight or nine new stragglers show up to replace those we've lost. They bring cases of beer, quarts of liquor, little curled-over baggies and aluminum squares of whatever. Nicotine light burns through every window, and from the parking lot Katie's building resembles a zoetrope moored in the dark.

As soon as everyone's good and loaded Dean produces an old wooden pickax from God-knows-where, and starts screaming for the fucking laptops. No one knows what he's talking about, and we all assume he's just being Dean. But there really are laptops, and Katie arrives about fifteen minutes later to prove it. I could give a good goddamn about some old busted laptops, however; for Katie Ludwick is wearing my jacket.

"It's my jacket," she says.

"Okay, it's your jacket. Can I have it?"

"What's going on?"

"We threw a party."

"I can see that," she says.

"Your note said do what I want."

She gives me a long, smoldering stare that masks her secret delight. She says, "You can have the jacket later. I'm cold."

Oh, to be in the jacket's proximity and yet not allowed within its snuggly embrace!

"Look what I found." Katie opens the cardboard box, revealing three black notebook computers. None of them work. I manage to stare into the box while continuing to leer at the jacket. Katie screams, "Take the damn box, I'm pregnant."

Oh yeah. I hold the laptops like an archaeologist might hold the tooth of a dinosaur. "Where are they from?"

"I stole them."

"From where?"

"I can't believe you guys decided to do this here."

"We figured you'd be too pregnant to go anywhere else."

Dean rushes up behind me, sticks his red wirebrush beard into the box, and snatches forth a clunky old Thinkpad. He raises it to the sky. He taps the head of his pickaxe against the concrete, and slowly a crowd gathers 'round.

We grant Adam the ceremonial first toss. Dean at bat. He swings the pickax just like Mickey Mantle, and the laptop splits into two pieces, screen-side and keyboard-side, before it ever hits the ground.

How broken can something get? When you can obliterate a computer without applying more than the slightest amount of force, what else is left to break?

The beauty is that these things were already broken long before tonight.

We survey the initial decapitation. Is this broken enough? No. It can break so much more. In this state—long before this state—the machine will no longer function. From this point, every subsequent descending level of destruction only describes how much difficulty will be involved in putting it all back together. Like Dante's levels of Hell: before you even reach Hell you are dead, the body is no longer functional, but down you go. The user says the machine is broken. The user does not care how broken it is, he just wants it fixed. But the technician knows. This is his trade. The priest knows how desecrated a body can possibly become and how difficult that will make his job in preparing the spirit for death.

Dean hands the axe over to Adam. We find joy in crushing the computers, every one of us connected to modernity's threat of the "rising machine"—the fear of domination by our own creation. But man made the pickaxe as well.

At one point a great blow tears the CD-Rom drive from the chassis, and a Microsoft Windows disk is ejected like a driver through the windshield.

Silence descends for one brief moment. We all gather 'round. The disk is already broken. A piece of it has snapped off. The disk is completely useless. *Smash it*, we say. *Break it*, we say.

We pass the axe around. Some, drunk to the point of emotional assimilation with the tool, must be forcefully separated from it to give others a turn.

"The candy! Be careful of the candy!" Dean shrieks. He runs around, fingers aflame in his blaze of hair, and this becomes the mantra of the evening. "Don't break the candy."

But this digital piñata exposes only further levels of itself, deeper layers of brokenness. There are capacitors, circuit boards, transistor chips, plastic fan blades, wires, latches, screws. There are strips of plastic and rubber: items no one expected to see squirting out of such polite and sterile machines. Copper sheets crumple and writhe. Who expected so many moving parts? Peripherals, magnets, perfectly polished silver disks— no one can figure out what these are for. Cylinders. Objects of beauty and symmetry, tiny works of art hiding within. Bits that do nothing but direct the flow of energy.

But there's still so much more to break.

The CPU pops out. Smash it. There is nothing recognizable inside. Like the human brain it is globular and homogeneous. Such a sharp contrast with the viscera. The viscera make sense like plumbing makes sense. Messy as it is, you can point out, *yes here, this fits here and digestible matter flows from here to here where it sits. Here, this place is where the nutrients are extracted. Yes...* But the brain? Nothing but pulp. No place to say: *Thoughts flow from here to here and are analyzed here.* Nothing like that. And the processor chip is nothing like that either.

The chip is senseless, gutless, black-grey matter.

We're onto the third laptop and it seems as though we've been swinging for ages. Going after little pieces like storks after crickets. Missing more than striking now, blasting chips from the street. Can it be broken still further? Transistors are severed. The keys of a keyboard, little helmets popped off of pogo hammers that close a local circuit. Between this are layers of rubber and thin plastic. The screen itself reveals multiple levels of translucence. One clear slip comes loose and is picked up, held up to a streetlight. The image fades to infrared on one side, ultraviolet on the other.

Our tone is a juggler's patch: menacing, vindictive, and playful. Striking with laughter. Be careful of the candy! Down with the fucking machines. "You ate my homework," someone cries, cursing the hard drive.

The batteries were removed before smashing began. For safety perhaps, or for ceremony—symbolizing the swift clean death offered by a civilized society. Machines have their batteries removed all the time. Go to sleep. Go to sleep. Anesthetized, the laptop has no clue how many levels of brokenness it descends.

There is silence. The pickaxe falls onto a patch of grass. Dean scans the parking lot with wobbly eyes on his wobbly head. I notice Adam out there digging among the shrapnel, occasionally holding some broken part up to the light, looking for God-knows-what. Three laptops in tatters, eviscerated along the gravel. Thousands of pieces, bits and scrap from one corner of the old lot to the other—cracked, smashed, mangled.

"I'll put it all back together in the morning," slurs Dean, raising his bottle. "I'll glue it and duct tape it together. Save all the pieces. Don't lose any of the pieces! It'll be a work of art. A goddamn sculpture. I'll take some glue and fit it all in place and pretend it works. Think of how it'll look. The fucking screen is split in two! I'll put some duct tape right across the middle. I'll wrap it in string. I'll carry it to a class and pretend to take notes. I'll bring it into a systems technician and tell them it just stopped working—see if they'll diagnose. I'll do this with a straight face. I don't know what's the problem, I'll say. I'm no good with these things, I'll say. I'll send it back on warranty. It just died, I'll say. I don't know what happened. It was fine the other day and then suddenly it just stopped working."

6.

By the third beer run, an utter failure due to the typical alcohol laws that apparently no one at the party remembered, those of us not homeward bound or passed out on some coffin-sized segment of the floor no longer concern ourselves with clocks, causality, or coherency. The conversations crawl one over another like a colony of ants. All that remains is the tip of the tongue, the unleashing of everything unspoken during daylight hours.

People say things like:

"I don't enjoy oral sex—giving or receiving. I find it demeaning and impersonal."

"Well it's no handshake."

"I'm serious."

"It lacks the subtlety of a high five."

Tears and hugs accompany reckless kisses, tangled theories, rotten jokes. The conversations weave in and out and the word flows sloshing and sluggish from the resplendent lips of youth.

For instance:

"We're leaving for tomorrow in two days!"

And...

"I want to be the guy who—you know, the guy in

a little Japanese village with the old man who fights spiders."

"I want to be the guy who tells the same old story over and over."

And...

"Mila used to own a rat. She'd bring it into bars because it loved to drink."

"I love strawberries after sex. It's like rewarding yourself for having a good time."

And...

"What would you do if you won a million dollars? I tell you what I'd do. I'd hire two private detectives to follow each other around."

Someone says, "Did you see the party goat? That goat gets puked on more than any other goat in this history of goats," while someone else is saying, "I want to...I want to be the guy who tells stories about flying badgers."

I hear the question, "Aren't you an organ donor?"

And then the reply, "No, I still have to get it changed on my license."

And then, "You know it just means they won't try as hard to save you."

Among the chatter, Will arrives. He and Dean and I sit down to pour overflowing shots and discuss the secrets of the universe. For a short time there is a lull in the conversation, and we stare quietly into the fire at pulsing portals to red dimensions and little black worlds in the coals. A big log splits in the middle, crashing down in two pieces, crushing our visions. Dean and I gasp. We must have looks of complete devastation on our faces because Will flails his arms in mock panic and says, "Oh no! Our burning structure has collapsed into a burning structure. There's flames and debris everywhere, just like it was before," which puts things into perspective, and makes me wonder why among of all the zillions of chemical combinations in all the billions of galaxies out there, humans became so antagonistic toward disorder.

Dean seems to emerge from a coma. He slurs his words. "Lost among the lost, we are scattered yet unified in this tide. Clinging to driftwood splintered from the same tree. Each one of us a unique carved-out canyon of DNA through which the same great ocean finds temporary diversion. Glancing out the corners of our eyes. Tracking potential lovers, rivals, or one-night stands."

An unbroken chain of desire's flame and the extinguishing satisfaction.

The frenzy of generations, the distributed orgy of time—throwing ourselves against this mill of longing to be ground by Kali's teeth into food for our children. Sex-slaves performing at the whim of future generations, lured on by our descendents. Possessed to passion by spirits longing to exist. Here and now procreation remains a mash of conflict, a dizzying delightful head-on collision of confusion, but I have seen the schematics of our great great unborn grandchildren tugging at our strings. Tributaries from distant possible futures, spawning upstream as time flows backward toward our ancestors.

When the words fray hopelessly past the point of coherency, Dean conducts one last toast. "To the little baby Katie and her little baby baby," we cheer.

7.

Dean and I pull each other up and stumble into the living room. There we find Katie Ludwick in perfect posture on the couch, snug in our jacket. Her lips part without making a sound. Her eyes full of horror. Adam is there beside her, down on his knees, yammering like a radiator with a loose gasket. He holds aloft a small silver disk with a hole in the center like a washer. It occurs to me that maybe this is some gizmo that flew out of one of the laptops. One of the pieces Adam was picking through earlier. Something flat and metallic. More than one witness to the event insists that this is supposed to be like a wedding ring. Others posit that this is precisely what Adam wants us to think. Either way, there's no stopping him until the pressure drops. His words pour forth in a torrent, crashing against the sides of his mouth, ricocheting off his lips like he's been carrying them around all these months. As if he composed every word the night she kicked him out and has just been waiting for the right moment to release them. They are the words of a man on his deathbed uncorking his soul. I don't know if it's the alcohol or the alignment of the stars, but his voice bears neither desperation nor doubt. He says what he says because it has to be said, not because he thinks it will make a damn bit of difference. I only wish I'd heard it from the beginning.

8.

"—and in my imagination I erase all the stupid things I've ever told you, and we...and we get to start over and meet again for the first time. I pretend it happens at a party like this one. I come around the corner and there you are. Our eyes lock long enough to get past whatever it is that keeps people from really connecting to each other. You know, that specific amount of time where the brain panics and people get nervous and look away. But we stare too long and too deep for strangers, too long even for friends. I see us standing there and shaking hands and not letting go, and the whole time our bodies count the seconds while we can't look away. I say, I'm Adam, and you say, I'm Katie. Hi, I say. Hi, you say—all the while with our eyes reflecting back on each other, like a hall of mirrors, penetrating stupidly into the depths. Thoughts bouncing back and forth between our eyes even faster than pheromones. Oh Katie—see? You're looking at me like that now. This is what I'm talking about. This is a reason for us to need each other. And in my imagination we both try to get back in, to regain eye contact, to see if we can beat the record. But... but here's the problem, see... You and I, we're competition. We're a threat to all the failed love affairs in history, and they're all conspiring to keep us apart...Then for whatever reason I suddenly have to leave the party, but you find a way to become my ride home. The universe fights back. The universe always fights back, but we beat the odds. We end up going back to my apartment. It doesn't matter that you don't have a car. It doesn't matter that I don't have an apartment. I've pre-imagined the apartment I would have, all down to the last detail. I invite you in and all we do is talk, but not a lot. Not as much as I usually talk. You talk more than I do, because—you know—because I'm nervous and I love the sound of your voice. You're making your way from room to room, getting a drink, clearing off the table, sometimes kneeling beside me to show off your latest zine or some art from your backpack. Look—you say—look I cut up this old shirt and made a dress out of it. That's one thing you say, and I think it's pretty great. I keep trying to catch your eye again, but neither of us push it. We sit on the floor beside the couch, and you tell me about your mother. You tell me about the first Madonna cassette you bought, and a little story about something that happened in high school. It's a good story and I laugh and spend a few minutes thinking about it. You ask me if I'd like to hold hands, maybe just for a minute, just to see how it feels. How does it feel? I imagine how it feels—I remember how it feels. Our fingers interlock and fit. All fingers interlock and fit, right? That's the universe trying to stop us. Okay, yeah, but not like this, I think. Look at these hands, Katie. Do you remember how good we fit? *Do you want to kiss me?* you ask, and stupidly I reply, *Can I?* And... and you find my reply somewhat endearing so you don't respond— but then I kiss you anyway, holding your face with one

hand, and I am warm and thundering. And it's like…
it's like…it's like lightning or something splits a tree
and the sparks set the forest floor on fire. Oh God, we
didn't expect that. But we ride it out…we ride it out…
it's like we're trying to find that precise amount of eye
contact where there's no going back. We feel each other
out, but you refuse to lose control. There are so many
reasons not to lose control. Not for someone like me, not
for someone who doesn't have an apartment or a job or a
future. Not for someone so strange and so reckless. You
know that you need to be careful in choosing a mate. You
can stop this, you think, but then you start to imagine
me in tears, heartbroken. You feel like all hearts are
fated to break, and you're worried that you'll break
mine and that I'll feel it all the way down because I love
you so much, and maybe I won't ever stop breaking.
You worry that maybe I'll just keep trying to make it
work, to get you back, to overtake you—but you won't
submit. You can't submit. The universe has eyes everywhere. Now I'm outside your window and you can hear
me saying: Don't go. Don't go. I need you. Or…I want to
need you. Am I supposed to need you or not? I mean, am
I supposed to be aloof or adoring or what? I'm just who I
am, Katie, and I know none of these words make sense
to you, either in my imagination or in reality, but this
is where I fit. You are where I belong. However I try to
imagine it, however the scenario goes down in my head,
I'm always back under your window begging for you to
take me back. You are more beautiful than all the first
winter nights. You're like those little crystal snowlets
when it hasn't even snowed yet—that just hang in
the air and dangle on spider webs. You're the kind of
sunset that causes shipwrecks. You're a crystal ocean
washing up to the shores of a red desert where the moon

is bigger than the sun and albino lions stand on a mesa surrounded by vineyards of gypsum…and…and…and Katie, when I'm old and in a rocking chair, and I look to my right I know I will see your face, whether you're there with me or not."

CHAPTER FIVE

RIVER

Missoula, MT

And then there was the time I rescued the girl from the pit.

Seriously, public works had dug a massive hole out of a street corner somewhere in the U district. I guess they were trying to get to a pipe problem, but it was going to take longer than they originally thought, so they blocked it off with saw horses, police tape, plastic fencing, and nasty notes. The pit sat there all weekend just waiting for lovely ladies to climb down inside.

She was Japanese and ninety-nine different kinds of adorable. I was on a walk and I just happened to glance over the warning signs and into the hole, because that's the kind of thing I can't resist. I thought I would just gaze into this neighborhood anomaly and ponder the pipes and guts and tendons—the unearthed secrets of urban reality. Instead, I gazed into a pair of enormous eyes lashed by fawning silver streaks.

"Hello there," I said. She was sitting down.

"Hi."

"What are you doing?"

"Oh you know, just sitting around. In this pit."

She was beautiful. Normally I don't tell women they are beautiful when I first meet them, because they have a tendency to run away. But this girl wasn't going anywhere. "You're beautiful," I said.

"Thanks," she said. "I bet you say that to all the girls

you find trapped in pits."

I asked her what she was doing down there. Turns out she was just curious about how cold the dirt was at that depth and she had to find out. She'd crawled down, and like the proverbial cat in the tree, discovered it was not as easy to get back up. She was wearing all white, too. She must care a lot about strata temperatures, I thought.

"How long have you been down there?"

"Oh about an hour," she said.

"And no one's found you?"

"No one looks in holes anymore. You and I are a dying breed."

I looked around for something she could grab onto. There really isn't much lying around in residential neighborhoods that can be used to rescue girls from pits. I could have gone down in there with her, but then we might both be trapped. She told me the dirt down there was very crumbly and also very cold. Then I remembered that peasant revolts are won with gardening tools. When necessary, hammers and sickles double as weapons. The point is—every house on every block has a tool shed or a garage.

"Listen," I said. "I'm not trying to get into a philosophical discussion while you're stuck down there, but isn't it interesting? If Missoula was ever invaded all these people could rise up with their shovels and lawn mowers and chain saws."

"Sure, but everyone in Montana has guns anyway," she said.

"Good point."

"You know, this would be an awesome conversation to have around, say, coffee... somewhere on, say, top of the street."

I told her I'd be right back and ran down the block, looking in everyone's yard for a rake or something. The block was surprisingly tidy. Not a tool left over; everything locked up tight in the sheds.

On the next block I saw what I needed. Someone had left a garden hose snaked out over the lawn. Now all I had to do was a bit of breaking and entering. Trembling a bit I opened the gate. I considered knocking to ask permission, but then whoever answered would want to get involved with the rescue, and I didn't feel like sharing the glory. I crept over to the spigot and released the hose.

It was more than enough for the job. She only needed that little extra. She grabbed the hose and in two mountaineering steps she was out.

"I suppose I should give you my number," she said, gazing up at me through the euphoria of newly found freedom, "so I can buy you lunch or something to thank you."

"It was nothing," I said.

"So..."

She teetered on her heels. "You know, I had this weird thought while I was waiting for you to rescue me. I kind of expected for our eyes to lock the moment I reached the top, and when you looked you'd see a certain sparkle there. And that I'd see a certain sparkle in your eyes too. And those sparkles would cross paths and meet in the middle, between our faces, and like, high five or something, creating a big booming sparkly hypnotic moment fluttering around our heads."

"But that didn't happen?"

"Not really," she ran her fingers through her hair and spun a full circle on her toes, staring up at the clouds. Then she moved toward me, her hands groped the air just a few feet from my chest. "But there certainly is something about being rescued from a pit. Triggers a primitive response in the brain. Savage. Sexy."

"You should go with that," I said.

"I don't know," she said, "I think I'm a little too grateful. It's risky to base relationships on obligation."

"Relationship?"

"I'm just not comfortable feeling beholden. You wouldn't respect me for it later."

"Beholden?"

"How about this," she said. "It's a small world. Let's go our separate ways, and when fate brings us together the time will be right."

That sounded reasonable to me, and exciting. She hugged me and scurried off into the wooded rural wilderness. I never saw her again.

1.

The morning after the party I wake up on top of the washer and dryer. A trail of bodies leads from the basement into Katie's apartment, where anything slightly lumpy has been requisitioned as a pillow. Stuffed animals, balled-up sweaters, a towel wrapped around a dictionary. They huddle under the dozens of blankets Katie keeps on reserve. They share couches, chairs, and beanbags. They squeeze onto the great oval rug in the center of the floor like castaways on a raft.

I find Adam snoring in the bathtub.

Katie is awake, sitting on the front porch reading the Independent and drinking coffee.

"Hey," I say, rubbing my face.

"Baby's first bender," she says.

"They're all dead in there. You killed them."

"I know, they were annoying," she says.

"What are we going to do with the bodies?"

"Fuck it."

Back inside I consider making breakfast. I count seventeen passed-out patrons, but I'm certain there must be more curled up in the strange nooks of the apartment. Too much work, I decide, and put on another pot of coffee instead.

One by one they come back to life in various states of consciousness. Reluctant good mornings and woeful proclamations of hangovers accompany shuffling steps. Katie starts a pan of hash browns. I wonder why we have to worry about food every single day. Wouldn't it be more efficient if everyone just spent all Saturday eating to store up for the rest of the week?

"Killer party."

"I wish I remembered it."

"What happened to the goat?"

No one mentions Adam's declaration of love. We all do a pretty good job pretending it never happened. When he finally emerges from the bathroom the look on Adam's face is devastated, terrified. He talks to us about his dreams and the few things he remembers from last night, avoiding the obvious. He constantly glances at Katie like he expects her to come over and hit him in the head with a giant hammer.

After a few minutes Katie brings Adam a cup of coffee and he thanks her. She stands beside him as he takes a sip. "Too hot?" she says. "A little," he says. "Need any sugar or anything?" she says. "It's perfect," he says.

She doesn't walk away. She seems to stare at his elbow. He continues sipping and does not cease these little routine slurps because the minute he takes a break from the coffee he knows he will have to acknowledge the fact that she is standing right there, and he will have to look at her or maybe say something. When the cup is dry he keeps pretending to drink until all the attention in the room has turned away from him, and then he looks up at Katie and whispers, "That was good coffee," and she takes the cup and leads him into the kitchen. I can hear them talking in low, serious voices, but I can't make out a word.

2.

In the days that followed Adam began to drop by the house from time to time. His visits were always brief, five or ten minutes tops. Most of the time he talked to us as a group, then took Katie aside for a few private words before leaving. Amelia bluntly antagonized him, demanding to know why Katie should even consider taking him back.

I spent too much of my time chasing the jacket. It turned out that on the night of the party Katie put the jacket in the closet. Dean, drunk out of his mind, grabbed it and used it for a pillow. Then he took it home with him when he left. I could have screamed, but I let it go. Give it time. All jackets come to those who wait. But when I went over to his place to get it Katie had already recovered it. The jacket bounced around like this a few times. Even Adam ended up wearing it around for a day, but he seemed so anxious about Katie that I couldn't bear to take it away from him. Later when I asked him for it he said he left it at Dean's. I gave up, and decided to let the jacket chase me for a change.

All the while, Katie's belly expanded. I waited for her to fill the entire apartment.

According to the doctor she was three weeks away. She slept all the time. Then, one Sunday morning, Katie

Ludwick wakes me up with a tap on the head and says, "Let's go fishing."

I tell her she's too pregnant to fish. She tells me to shut the hell up. She holds her rod and hands me her fishing vest and says she has her dad's car for the weekend and she's going to use it. She hasn't gotten to fish all summer and by the time the baby's born and she goes through all the postpartum blah blah blah and settles down to the reality of this living creature, at least to the point where maybe she'll be willing to leave it in her mother's care for more than five minutes, the rivers will be too low and fishing will be for shit.

"I don't think leaving town is really such a good idea," I say.

"It's the best idea," she says. "It's the only idea."

I ask her what she plans on doing if she suddenly goes into labor.

"Then my kid will be born in the woods and I won't have to register her into society. She'll be a non-existent baby just like her non-existent daddy."

"It isn't safe. What would your doctor say?" I ask.

"She'd tell me not to ask stupid questions," Katie says. "You go get my brother. I'll pick up Amelia. Meet us at Butterfly and we'll leave from there."

"I was going to go down to the library," I say.

"Don't you know it's against the law in Montana for single women to go fishing alone?"

"Fine," I say. And that settles it.

Las Vegas, NV

The weeks between the morning when Melanie left me for good and the day I caught that Greyhound back to Missoula will always remain a blur, hard enough to piece together in my mind, even harder to put into words. But the last time I saw her face is as clear and present to me now as my own surroundings.

I followed her out of her apartment. I carried her accordion for her. She kept saying things from the doorway. "You were meant to be a spark in a million eyes, not a furnace in one," she said. "And I need something stable," she said, "someone I can rely on." My mind ignored her as it looped an endless mantra: *This is it*. A singular moment with no context, as adrift as raw existence itself. *This is it*. Staring at her ass without lust or emotion, as she dragged the small suitcase down the stairs, toy wheels thumping with each step. *This is it*. The zipper on the side-pouch half open, and nothing I could have done to stop her.

I am familiar with so many processes of decay, so many systems that break down through natural step-by-step means, that the loss of love feels like hypnotism or a cruel joke. Sometimes things just go away.

In those final moments she was a boutique display,

posed on the other side of the passenger seat window. She got in his truck and closed the door, leaving me standing there in the Vegas swelter. After a few seconds the truck rolled forward, window frame dragging her into the desert and out of my life. Gone for good and forever. All that remained were the imprints she left in my mind. I'll never forget that last look we exchanged through semi-tinted glass, blending us beyond any touch—her on the inside snug in a seat belt, me standing outside, sweating, unable to move.

The reflection of my face in the window superimposed across her face beyond it—closer than we'd ever been in real life, close enough for each to be the other. And then one last look of horror as she let herself realize this was it. Her eyes in my head, my lips on her chin, our hair tangled flat and colorless in the glass.

It. That's what this was.

She left with her eyes still in my head. And I saw everything the way she must have been seeing it for weeks.

My lips on her chin. Her face in my face. Was she trying to swap reflections and leave herself one last thing to come back for? Like all the little bits and ribbons left in my pockets over the weeks before, the buttons and receipts in my backpack.

We were a tangle long before that window got between us.

The first time I noticed was after hot sex in a hot shower. She got out to dry her hair and I stood there with the last of the water drizzling down my back. I looked down at my knees and I saw her toes. Her toes growing out of my knees. I jumped out of the shower to show her but by then they were back on her feet. Later that night I kissed her shoulder and when I pulled back my lips stayed behind. My fingers, tangled up in her hair, detached. She left her ear on my chest one morning like a pillow mint. Before long I found myself reaching for things I didn't even like. A jar of green olives in the fridge. Only her fingers had ever reached for green olives, not mine. She started to whistle, absently one day while reading a book. She could never whistle before. I began twirling my hair, or was it her hair? She pointed out the sort of things only my eyes had ever noticed.

So that day in the window was really nothing new. Our faces snagged together and caught up on the glass. In the mingled reflections she seemed to be wearing my lips. She was telling me with my own lips how complete the end this was about to be in five short seconds, four, three...leaving her eyes in my head...two, one, a gunning engine...zero. Some overwhelming desire had driven her to that moment, and then she was gone. The truck began to roll, leaving me in a cloud of dust, and she was gone.

To this day I don't know what she took with her and what she left behind. My thumbs seem smaller. I'm pretty sure.

3.

I haven't really hung out with Dean since the party. He lives about a mile east of Katie. The sun is swatting clouds out of its face and I can hear the river mingle with the murmur of pedestrians. Dean's small first floor apartment looks like a vacancy with its empty porch and dark windows. I drum my fingers on the door.

No answer. I knock louder. Still nothing. I try the handle but it's locked. I run around to the side-door. Also locked. I rest my ear up against the glass and I can hear voices inside. I hear the beep of an answering machine. The voices continue.

When I come back around to the front porch his door is slightly ajar. I can see a brass chain measuring the dark gap. "It's me," I say. The door closes, the chain comes down and Dean lets me inside.

The answering machine beeps again. "Why are your lights off?" I ask.

Dean shushes me, slumps down in his couch. He grabs the answering machine off the coffee table and sets it in his lap. We listen to the message. I recognize the voice. It's his ex-wife. He presses rewind and we listen to it again:

"Don't get me wrong, Dean, please don't. You have to understand if it were in any way possible for me to have avoided this call, to have not had to track down your number—a process that, by the way, took eleven days and required going out for 'drinks' with Max Kessler—I would have. My God, Dean, and it's not that I didn't want to talk to you, but I have come to understand, to fully comprehend your revulsion at the very idea of me, much less the possibility of having to share the same airspace as me and endure what may be an endless stream of thoughts, emotions, and confessions. But—and when I say but, please keep in mind that I am not trying in any way to be contrary or to start a veritable war of words—but I have had no choice. I've wanted to call you for months now, even longed for it from time to time, yet I have had this whole while what I felt was a choice. And that choice was grounded upon what I considered to be a well-developed respect for your feelings. Yes, Dean, your feelings, believe it or not, are a presence to me, and like a seed that a gardener plants and leaves to the elements, out of sight out of mind they say, but which finally germinates and sprouts and can no longer be ignored, a full appreciation for your emotional investment has at last come to light, and despite my own compulsions, and even *need* from time to time to visit you and impose upon you whatever ferocious manifestations of ovulation might have on any particular day reared its proverbial ugly head, I did not. I refused. I put your feelings first. Something that perhaps I never once did while we were, as it were, 'together' has become the absolute foundation for determining my own actions in this situation. And Dean, the situation has changed.

"Please don't erase this message until you've heard me out. There are things... important things... all I need right now is to know that you have been in earshot while I say these things. Dean, I know you won't believe me, but I really was in love with you. Truly I was. I didn't even know it then maybe, but I've come to realize, which just makes everything I did to you even worse. The point is—God, what is the point? Alright, here's the point… No. It's no use to tell you any of this, not even for my own benefit. I had some vague romantic notion of purging, of pushing out the gunk and the shit, but really there's too much. There's the me with the guilt, and there's the me that wants you to fall in love with me again so I can laugh in your face and call you a little boy and walk out, and there's the me who wants you to fall in love with me again so that I can kiss your sweet lips, swallow my own poison and die. There's the practical me, there's the slap in the face, there's the angry, there's the hurt, there's the possessed, there's the giddy and the girly. I've got—no, look, I'm trying to speak clearly. I should have just sent you a letter. And to think I'm running away again. I am, you know. I'm moving very far away and you'll never see me. And the thing is I have a child, Dean, and she's yours. You're thinking how could I possibly know that, and you're right, but I do. I know it like I know my own name. And it kills me that you'll never know her. But I can trace it all back and it makes sense, and I knew at the time. I could feel it taking hold when it happened. I could feel your spirit rushing into me. But I took everything from you, didn't I? I took everything and you're just a shell now and I'm moving away and I can't care what happens to you. I can't, but I do, but not enough to do anything about it. I don't know why I even called, really, but you had to know I suppose. And now it's done, I've said exactly nothing I planned on saying, so… bye."

4.

Dean goes to play it a third time. I ask him how long he's been sitting here listening to that message. Since yesterday, he says. I can't think of any suitable way to respond to that, so I tell him we're going fishing.

"Sounds fun," he says.

"No, see, you have to come with us."

"I can't," he says.

"Why not?"

"I can't leave."

"Why not?"

"I can't ever leave," he says.

"Ever?"

"I have everything I need. I've been preparing for this moment."

I check out his kitchen. The fridge is full of gallon-jugs of water and ketchup bottles. Bags of frozen blueberries in the freezer. His cupboards burst with non-perishables: cans of fruit, beans, bags of rice, wheat-free noodles, tomato sauce. There's soup, soup, and more soup. Chocolate bars in every drawer.

"You can't stay here forever," I say. "Your sister wants you to go fishing with her."

"We'll never make it across town."

"She's going to have a baby soon. You want to be there for that, right?"

"That's another thing," he says. "How does a virgin get pregnant? It's impossible. The child is an implant. All of them are. A rising generation born to bury us."

Dean presses play. I grab the answering machine out of his hands and make it stop. He whimpers a little but does not protest. "Seriously, how long have you been sitting here listening to this?"

"Only a few days."

"She's just fucking with you. She knows what buttons to push. I doubt any of it's true."

"It's all true," he says. "Everything is true. I'm under surveillance. They're using her to scare me into the open." I remember the time Dean daydreamed Romanian spies into old Coupe de Villes, and pointed out eighty-year-old ladies with cameras in their eyelids.

"That's stupid," I say.

He looks at me with horrible wide eyes that slowly narrow into suspicion like pupils contracting in the light.

"Jacket," I say. "Where's your jacket?"

I'd almost come to terms with the fact that I would never see the jacket again, much less wear it—but now the need is desperate. This is the moment, goddammit. I run around the apartment looking everywhere.

"On the microwave," he tells me at last.

I return to the living room, holding it in my hands. I can feel its cuddliness nuzzling into my fingertips. I hold it up to Dean's face. "See this? Do you know why I've wanted this so badly? It keeps you invisible from classified technology."

Dean gives me that look. Crazy people aren't stupid and they know when you're patronizing them. "Fine," I relent. "But it'll still keep you warm. Come on, you don't have a choice. The pregnant lady demands it."

I can see the gears whirring in his head; see his brain trying to mesh his sister's desires in with his current picture of reality, looking for a way to reconcile. Whatever it is that finally makes the link exists so far inside his mind I probably wouldn't have understood even if he'd explained it. "Yes," he says. "We have to go. But we have to go the secret way."

"Okay, okay," I say, helping him into the jacket. "Secret way it is."

"Zozezaz," he whispers under his breath.

5.

We leave the house and I let him lead. I'm jealous he gets to wear that jacket. It's just so damn comfy. We cross Orange Street, head north, and creep down into the park where we take shelter under the bridge. Shelter from what?

"The sky is a seamless dome of hexagonal mirrors," Dean says.

"Katie is waiting for us at Butterfly."

"We'll have to call her. Butterfly is not an option. And we can't cross the bridge. Too many passenger cars. Our only way over the river is the tracks."

There's an old unused railroad bridge about a half-mile north of us. Completely the wrong direction, but Dean's the boss. These old tracks run north and south through Missoula, and have been out of commission for years. They span the river between Broadway and a no-man's land filled with slouching fences and old abandoned buildings. Dean leads me under the railroad bridge and over a fence that explicitly tells us what shitty citizens we are for crossing it. We creep through a scorched and abandoned mid-century horse stable that I call the airplane hangar. We huddle in the dark and wait for invisible helicopters to fly past. Dean checks the perimeter. He picks up a rock and throws it out into the field, waiting to see what happens. Nothing happens.

Then we cross the tracks. Dean insists we touch no

rail or other form of metal in case they're monitoring this area via low-voltage conductive flow. So we hop from wooden plank to wooden plank. The grandfatherly old Clark Fork tumbles below in tiny turbines of lazy river water. Dean watches the sky.

Before you start thinking Dean is completely crazy, he's not. What he's going through today is a retreat into a safe place in his mind. It may not seem safe with all the hexagonal mirrors and spy cameras and government agents and Hopi witch doctors on his trail, but trust me—it's infinitely safer than the parts of his mind where his ex-wife still dwells. Paranoia takes Dean back to a more innocent world: television shows and marijuana, cops and robbers with the neighborhood kids, freaking each other out on the dark dash. A world of pre-defined tensions and resolutions. Some familiar territory, navigable only via coded pathways and personal incantations.

Once across, we don't turn toward town but continued north along a perpendicular set of railroad tracks. We push beyond the knapweed fields and trickle into the lovable Northside of Missoula. Northside: the neighborhood I most fondly remember for ogling over crystals of MSG as if it was a controlled substance. This section of town doubles as a museum for Old Industry—last century's booms, the rail, the wheel. Oil-hemorrhaging champions of transportation. Arrhythmic aberrations of night, and the things that truly go bump therein echo the deep bovine groans of machinery—the shudder and clash of the train cars, an occasional blast of steam, an eighteen-wheeler coming or going.

Dean grins for the first time. We press our backs into a giant rusting oil drum. A pay phone clings to the wall of a gas station on the far side of a gravel lot littered with crushed beer cans like land mines.

"I'm going to go for it," I say.

"Okay," Dean says.

"Unless you'd rather."

"I'll keep a lookout here."

I walk over to the phone booth, and baffled, I pick up the receiver. I need thirty-five cents now? Since when? I find the number for Butterfly and ask to speak with Katie.

"What's taking you so long?"

"This is weird," I say. "Who comes and empties out all the quarters?"

Katie sounds annoyed. "We need to get on the road."

"Dean's having a bad day," I explain.

"Well hurry up. The sun's getting high."

Per Dean's instructions I tell Katie to pick us up by the Interstate. I tell her we're going to pretend to be hitchhikers and Dean wants her to pull over as if we don't know each other and they've just decided to pick us up, and then we will get in the car. She laughs and hangs up the phone.

Dean and I wait by the on-ramp and he casts quiet spells on cars as they pass us. Some hippies in a van stop and ask if we need a ride. Dean tells them we already have one and sticks out his thumb.

Fifteen minutes later a white '77 Cadillac scraps into the gravel up ahead. We jog toward the single working break light. Amelia opens the passenger door and we crawl into the back seat. Adam is there, rolling cigarettes. "Hey guys, how are you?" He asks this in such a genuine fashion—I don't think small talk is even a concept he's aware of.

For some reason neither Dean or myself are able to answer this question. Finally Katie says, "They're fine."

My Ridiculous Childhood

I haven't yet mentioned my ridiculous childhood. I fell in love for the first time at age seven. Ha ha, you laugh. How cute. Puppy love. No. This was the real thing. Dead serious. From seven years old I chased this girl for two years with unwavering determination. I might be chasing her to this day had my parents not decided to move to Montana. I wrote epitomes of love, saved up for jewelry, I even sang a'cappella in an assembly room of parents and students and dedicated the song to her. A younger initiate into the dour secrets of the heart there never was.

This poor young thing never gave in to my advances, never returned more than friendship. Her name was Rachael. She was golden-haired and at least four inches taller than me. Later, once I'd resigned myself to the fact I would never have the girl, I turned severely from her type and I have pursued darker-haired ladies ever since. Not a single blonde has touched these lips. It took me about twenty-eight months to give up my pre-pubescent pursuit of Rachael. Oh how I pined. How many thousands of tears I wept. The vows I made to myself and to God, at a mere eight years old, swearing on my life never to love again, that if I could not have her then I would be the last of my bloodline—neither marriage nor children.

I wonder if I've damned myself to the chase. I try to trace my restless tendencies, my surges of romance and subsequent withdraw from intimacy, my inability to stay in one place for longer than a few months. Could it all come down to unrequited love at a tender age when most boys still think girls are infested with the plague? If Montana rescued me from my earliest passion it's no wonder I continue to use her this way, to trust her to resolve all conflicts.

Occasionally I still get a glimpse of that seven-year-old me hiding deep in my brain, pulling his homuncular levers. Childhood is a secret whispered into the ear that we spend the rest of our lives trying to remember.

6.

Katie Ludwick turns off at Bonner and follows Highway 200 toward a fishing spot she wants to try. Amelia's feet burden the dash. We all stare at the windows. The woods are bright and still. Afternoon is coming on, bugs are off to nap, and Katie grumbles about what a horrible time it is to go fishing.

We follow a narrow trail through the bushes, down to the river and a small bare embankment covered in white stones. Katie stands where the water slaps the dirt and where over the years a little shelf has formed. Amelia and I sit among an intricate system of tree roots, bunched up in the shade. Dean stares into dangling leaves. Adam keeps rolling cigarettes for Amelia and talking with everyone, a question here, a story there, gestures of affirmation for all.

The river is calm and shallow for several feet out until a swift and deep vein bubbles up a cascade of ripples. Katie will fish just inside of those ripples. She puts on her waders, assembles her pole, and ties a fat fly to the end of her line. Downstream a ways four concrete pylons tower naked in a row from bank to bank. Steel rods and rims of rubble fray forth from the scalp of each crumbling monument. The bridge is gone but the pylons remain.

"I thought fish didn't bite at noon," Adam says. Katie tells him that he doesn't know anything and to just shut up and then she leans closer into his body and with one hand she holds his arm for balance and with the other she goops up her fly. Before she hits the river she rests her fingertips on his cheek and she kisses him. Her lips get lost in his beard, and I tell myself I knew this would happen even though part of me was scared that it wouldn't.

"Well," Amelia asks me. "Will you tell me about Vegas now?"

Adam and Dean are out of earshot, pointing out various plants and insects to one another. I watch Katie lift her rod to the sky. She sways on her ankles, rocking back and forth on the brittle shore. Her line catches in the breeze and she lets out a little extra. Steps into the river. Lets out a little more. She leans to the right, tilting the pole. Her fly snaps to attention and her line tugs into the wind.

And then, because I have nothing better to do, I tell Amelia everything. I tell her about finding out Vegas girl was dating someone else the whole time we were together. Some guy from Iowa. How I found this out was I ran out of money and got evicted and I had nowhere else to stay so I showed up at her place with my stuff. But the guy from Iowa was visiting her that week, too. Having nowhere else to go I stayed there that night, slept on her couch while he slept in her room. We were up until 3am trying to talk it out. A conversation dense with spaces sheltered our voices. She spoke in a light breeze, and I, a drop or two of rain. Communication going nowhere she slipped away to her room, leaving me with a pillow and a blanket. Even with her door closed I could hear them talking from down the hall. Their words meandered through the hollow house, reaching my ears as a distant foreign language. "Wellamso ab hilblim," she said. "Donfy leeba, yobofro Iyd," was his reply. These phrases dwindled to moans and sighs, the arrhythmic creaks of bedsprings against a syncopated thud of wood on wall.

I tell Amelia how I survived the night by remembering that Dean once lived with his ex-wife and her boyfriend for two whole months. The next morning I moved into a hostel near the Strip and recoiled from the shock. Found my balls again. But then she found me in a coffee shop and gave me the whole story. I guess she'd been in love with this Iowa guy since high school. I always thought ours was the epic romance, but theirs transcended everything. Years of struggles and back and forth, and him never making a real commitment, always traveling around the country, visiting to sweep her off her feet every few months before dashing off again. He was her true love but it could never work, and besides he'd lit out for North Carolina or something. She told me she'd broken up with him for good this time. She wanted to be with me now. There are three or four women in the world to who I am able to say 'no' only until they ask. For one more month we were happy. We hardly left her bed. I think mostly she felt bad for me because I was homeless in Las Vegas, though I'm sure she loved me in some small way. But when the guy from Iowa had a change of heart and drove up again in his truck she melted right under the door, dripped down the stairs, and seeped into his cab.

I tell Amelia how I ran after her. How I stood at the car window. Her hand on the glass. My face in her face. How the muffler coughed to life and she was gone.

"Oh, dear," Amelia says. She reaches over and takes

my hand and we stare into the river in silence.

Dean and Adam hold a large piece of driftwood between them. Just standing there holding it like two paramedics might hold a stretcher. They stare at each other. I see Adam's jaw moving. Always moving. Rhythmic, fatherly, story after story. He'll make an amazing dad.

"Anyway," I say at last.

"Yeah," says Amelia. She puts her fingers in my hair while she smokes with her other hand. "So what's next?"

I pause. Scratch my face and breathe all the air out of my lungs. This is the point where I usually don't say anything more. I stare at the palms of my hands, holding them empty in front of me. "I'm afraid," I say. "Afraid that if I keep moving around from place to place that I'll miss something crucially important that you don't get to see unless you just sit still for a long time. But I can't help it. Whenever I try to stay put I freak out that the rest of the world is moving on without me. I can't decide. I can't decide anything."

She grips the back of my neck and speaks in a low, soft voice. "The road is your rebellion against growing old. From our point of view you *are* the one standing still."

I watch Dean climb around the rocks. The jacket looks good on him. I'm convinced it keeps him safe. He seems calmer out in nature, trading in his worries for a jacket and a piece of driftwood. I can relate. Everything I want is here. Everything except that sweet longing to return.

Amelia stares at the soft pebble floor of the riverbank. She reaches into her purse. "Here," she says. She hands me a silver disc of polished aluminum. I recognize it immediately as that little ring of metal Adam found among the laptop guts the night of the party. I recall the way he held it up in front of Katie the whole time he was pouring his own guts out. Without pride or desperation. The ring feels almost liquid smooth between my fingers. I wonder what it was for.

"You couldn't even fit a pinky through this," I laugh. "Why do you have it?"

"They gave it to me in the car. Adam and Katie. He said he's going to get her a proper ring, but that this one belongs to all of us. I think you should hold onto it for a while."

Then she leans over and wraps her silver-sleeved arms around my neck, hanging onto me in that sideways way that makes it hard to hug back. We sit there for a long time until drained of unspoken words. Why do we do it? Why do we keep coming back to that place— prowling for each other, approaching strangers, kissing them—when we know, when we know, when we know, without any doubts, experientially we know, statistically we know, that it won't work out—that it can only end in pain and sorrow. We keep stepping onto the painted X, creeping into the trap, opening our hearts, undressing every layer, saying those same words—all the while echoes of the crash drift over our shoulders, whispering into our ears even as I whisper into hers.

"Really Joshua," she whispers back, "you always pick the strangest times to say these things."

7.

Katie is hip-deep now, well in the groove, blank-faced. Her casting harmonizes perfectly with the river breeze. Water splashes up against her round and perfect belly.

Dean walks over and shows us a bug that he is carrying around on a twig. He says, "All of us here right now, we are all cut from the same cloth."

Adam calls out to Katie, "How goes it?"

"Not one goddamn strike," she says.

We make sandwiches and spread them out on the smooth side of an old log. Dean keeps wandering off to speak to the bushes. Sometimes he refuses to open his eyes for minutes at a time because visual information is a construct imposed upon him, a fabrication by certain forces attempting to lead him into a false sense of self. When I ask if I can wear the jacket for a while he hugs it close to his chest.

Amelia stands up and lobs a few rocks into the river, trying to see if she can break it. Katie yells at her to stop, "You'll scare the fish."

"That is my intention," Amelia says. "I am a savior of fish."

Dean cues off of this and flings riverward a stone of his own. He stares at the point where ripples heal over the splash. He raises his arms high and they begin slowly to sway. His fingers wiggle in the wind and the river massages the shore. Dean is not defined by a career or a family or politics or a home; he is defined only by the music in the movements of his arms, arms which now sway in time with his sister's gentle casting. The sleeves on his jacket flutter like the wings of a caddis fly.

Katie is yelling back to us that she's just about ready to take a break when something flashes on the river. None of us saw it, but later on we will all swear that we had. Katie's line goes tight. Her wrists tense. Her rod becomes a question mark. Her leader a spotlight upon the surface of the waters.

"She's got one," Adam says.

"How big is it?" I say.

"Feels pretty big," Katie says. She looks like a Norse goddess with her blond hair blazing in the sunlight, arms held high as if holding aloft a spear or a bolt of lightning.

"Does she have a net?"

"Katie Ludwick needs no net!"

Dean stands on the stump of a tree and orchestrates the event, mimicking his sister's motions. I see his lips move: *Zozezaz.*

Katie's huge splashing steps toward shore alternate with moments utterly still. Sometimes she reels in a few clicks, other times she releases some line. Whenever she reels, Dean's fingers flare and stab outward like bear claws; when she lets go, his head bows over in weariness. When she shouts, his lips move: *Zozezaz.* Katie never releases more than she reels in. She adjusts

175

the tension on the line ever so slightly. The high tip of her rod is epileptic.

"It's pretty big," she screams. "Get my net!"

"Katie Ludwick needs no net," Adam says.

"You didn't bring one," I say.

"Yes I did, it's in my bag."

"No it isn't."

"Goddammit, look again!"

I look again. Her bag is empty.

"Goddammit. Goddammit!"

We all start to laugh—well, Adam and I do—Dean is still engaged in his sympathetic magic and Amelia ignores us to pick flowers. If I had a net I would gather them all up in one swoop, these spirits I've known for years and their ever-aging bodies. I'd place each of them in a town exactly like Missoula, in houses and apartments exactly like the ones they live in now, in relationships and problems and confusions no different from those they've been muddling through all their lives. I would put on Katie's jacket and leave them behind and follow the river to the mouth of the sea until my clothes were drenched and brambles tore into my flesh and my lungs filled up with water—then I would come back to find them all unchanged.

"Think it'll get away?" Adam asks.

"Hell no," I say.

"Goddammit," Katie shouts. This time her cries are a curse over the waters. "Goddammmmmmm!" The word catches in her throat and eases into a groan. For a brief instant I see the tip of her rod lower way too far and she seems to stagger, but the moment passes and she falls right back into form. But her groan doesn't stop. It grows louder and rises in pitch and becomes a wail.

"Is she okay?"

"Are you okay?"

"I'm going to have a fucking baby," she screams.

"It took her nine months to figure this out?"

"I think she means now," says someone, but I don't know who, for it's just at this very moment we all realize Katie Ludwick is going to have a fucking baby.

We fire off a series of questions, mostly for our own benefit. She volleys back with primal screams and obscure curses. Adam and I begin to run toward the bank, then stop. Dean yells, "She's got a big one!"

"Katie," Adam says. That and, "Hold on," is all he can think to say.

"Get out of the water," I say. "We'll drive you to the hospital."

"This goddamn fish is not getting away!"

Still, she continues taking slow steps toward shore, with something of a heightened sense of urgency. Dean's feet rise and fall in place. His skybound hands pull at the invisible taffy that gum us all to this moment in time.

"Is she seriously going into labor?" I say.

"I think so."

"What do we do?" Adam says.

"Be a man," says Amelia.

"Come out, Katie. Drop the rod!"

Katie Ludwick spares two seconds to look over her shoulder and give me a death glare that can only be interpreted to mean: *Go to hell or someplace similar. No baby is going to get between me and my life. The baby can wait. You dudes can wait. Fuck off.*

Dean grins, guiding his sister to shore. Amelia says, "We need a blanket." I literally run around in circles. Everyone starts talking at the same time. How did we not bring a blanket? Dean, get over here. Take off your jacket, my jacket, Katie's jacket—lay it down there. No, right there. Katie you have to get out of the water!

With the boxing jacket all spread out like an operating table, Amelia runs upstream to wash her hands. Adam empties the little ice chest and fills it with water. We stand there stupidly as Katie takes baby steps toward the shore, a reel here and a reel there. Her line is getting shorter all the time. Dean moves toward us, gazing away at the hills, arms stretched out to heaven. *Zozezaz.* He lowers his arms and the breeze kicks in; when he raises his arms again the breeze dies down.

One Katie Ludwick foot comes out of the water and slaps down on the shore. Katie demands Adam dump the water out of the ice chest and use it for a net. Amelia tells him don't you dare! She begins unsnapping Katie's waders. I stand there not knowing what to do. I see Adam sort of crouch down and hunch forward like his body's trying to help in ways his brain hasn't figured out yet. Katie's eyes are on the water. Dean starts to laugh. Katie's rod trembles like a tuning fork. She grips it until her knuckles turn white. I see the fish's head dart out of the water and then dive. Katie lets a few inches of line slip through her fingers and then holds fast. Amelia's hands support Katie's armpits. "Sit back slowly, there you go—Adam get up and help me—sit back on the jacket, Katie."

"I've got him," Katie says. "I've got this son of a bitch." She groans again. Her voice is a siren that drowns out the very roar of the river.

And then suddenly Dean is there standing in front of me. He's wrapped his hand around the spasming rod, and he pushes it into my chest like a bouquet of flowers. I stare at him stupidly. "Take it," he says. I realize that I am home for this reason and no other. "Take it,"

Amelia says. I am not here to escape or to recharge or to reminisce. I am back in Missoula to steady the rod so that Katie can have this mystery baby without giving up her life, and for one fleeting moment my wandering legs become a source of stability.

I cradle a length of the pole in both arms and catch the line as it begins to slip. Dean turns away from us to face the crumbling pylons. I can feel the fish struggle and give in alternating beats. Katie's fingers barely cling to the rod's cork handle. The fish leaps once more as if gasping for air. Katie's right leg still in the water as her body topples down the staircase of Amelia and Adam toward the jacket that serves as her blanket. For a second I am dazzled by the glare of the noonday sun as Dean seems to part the clouds, and the next thing I see is Katie's rod arc toward the river like the curve of the moon or a blind man kneeling down to pray.

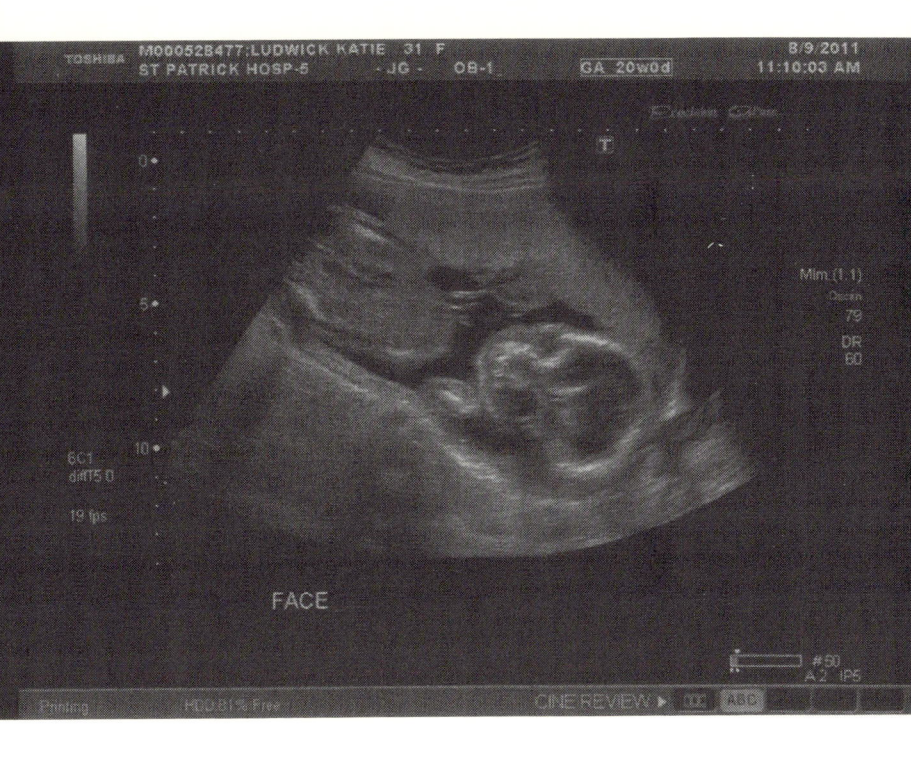

HIDDEN TRACKS

JOSHUA DEAN LUDWICK

GROWING SONG

by Katie Ludwick

faces denote the places
growing song

and I may be wrong
but I can feel your face
peeling back
scrunching back
I can feel your face
becoming a different face

the places we have been
all of them denote
a different melody
a different way of being
a different message
a different meaning

and in the song we all
have our own interpretation
whether it is philosophical
or rhythmic
whether it is mental
or physical

you dance about the room

and I wonder about
the placement
of a certain adjective
Does it change anything?

your face
my face
are they becoming one
in wonderment

thinking and knowing
so different
yet so similar

and I can't help
but wonder
when my idea
will become your dance
and vice versa
and we will roll
smiling
dancing
thinking
into the future.

Katie could tell your
     fortune
     watching spirals
 bloom from the creamer
in your coffee.

"Your future's all murky and
schwoogley!" she'd say.

TOMMY GALYEAN
Missoula Artist
1959 - 2003

RAIDING THE RITZ

(Another story of Katie Ludwick)

Originally Published in Slumgullion vol. 3, 2007

Katie said, "I want a beer," and that's what started everything.

Those four words triggered a countdown to our bizarre transformation from two disgruntled bastards on the sidewalk to beer revolutionaries looking for some way to gracefully set ourselves free from a coup that neither of us had entirely intended to unleash.

"Alright." I didn't know what else to say. We were both painfully aware there wasn't a stamp's worth of change between us. These were old broke days, old mooching days, long before the pregnancy, back when we dribbled through Missoula like sunstroke victims and survived on ramen, rice and Quaker oats. Back when "I want a beer," was more than just something to say; it was a call to arms.

"I have a dollar and a bunch of food stamps at home," Katie said.

The immediate solution, and one which had worked for us in the past, was to invite some poor sucker to buy us a six-pack. But we were barely in any mood for each other's company, much less some third party who may or may not subject us to endless accounts of their weekly highlights. By day's end we would find ourselves encroached upon by three-and-a-half dozen such scoundrels. But a mob is more tolerable to our ears than an individual. A mob makes a whole different sort of music. A mob rattles and consumes and gets shit done, and sound breaks from their lips in wordless raw ugly energy that tastes great with beer.

Katie and I had been sitting stupidly outside the Ritz for hours, backs against the old worn bricks. A great place to lean on a wall and watch the humans walk by. It was early—maybe about six. Not fifty feet behind us, inside the slick gloom of the bar, floated enough beer to drown the both of us. Delicious, overpriced, and entirely out of our reach. Knowing it was there warded off any other thoughts, leaving us slaves of proximity.

"I need a beer," Katie shouted to the air. Then she shouted it again. With each cry she shook her tiny fists at heaven and her vehemence intensified. I couldn't just sit there and let her suffer. And so, walking inside to take a piss, I began to scope the place out. Nine or ten customers, afterclockers, no one I knew well enough to bum a dollar from. There was only one bartender at the moment, bored out of his mind and watching the television. This was a Tuesday after all. If things were slow enough, and the bartender bored enough, he might just give us a beer; so I shuffled over and opened up the valve on my leaky faucet of charm.

"How about a free sample?"

"That's funny," the kid said. He was in his mid-twenties and wore short, sandy blond hair. Probably working his way through his last year of school. A busy man with no time for any of my nonsense. He kept staring at the TV and drying his hands on his pants.

"Come on," I persisted. "Half a pint of cheap beer in a plastic cup. What could it hurt?"

"It adds up. Who else wants free beer? Everybody. That's who."

Must be a Social Theory major. How was I to appeal to his better nature if he was only in this to win the argument?

"How about a trade? Would you make a trade?"

He looked over at me for the first time. "Yeah. I'll trade you a beer for three bucks."

Christ, this kid was a riot!

I kept trying to whittle him down, break his resolve, certain that at some point it would no longer be worth his time to endure my nagging, and he'd give me some beer just to go away. To his credit, this prick was stalwart. A second bartender came in a few minutes later, a big beefy guy with curly hair who'd never learned how to smile. "What do you think?" said Blondie. "Should I give this guy a free beer?"

"No," said Curley. And that was that.

"I knew you'd get nothing," Katie said when I was back outside. "It's useless."

"Do you want to go?"

"I'm too lazy. Let's just sit here."

"Alright," I said, and so we sat there, thirsty, sober, and silent.

Ten minutes or so later a friend of ours happened by, but there was less chance he had money than that money would fall from the sky. Bosco Howe, a buoyant leprechaun of a lumberjack—the first guy to ever hand me a pipe and say, "hit that"—eventually grew up to brew beer. I can't help but wonder how much the day's events at the Ritz contributed to his path.

Bosco stopped and said hello. I squinted up into the sun, and like a true friend, I asked him if he had any money.

And, like a true friend, he did not.

"Katie needs a beer," I said.

In those days Katie dressed a little like Janis Joplin. She had on this baggy muumuu sort of thing, a dozen necklaces, and round red-tinted sunglasses. Orange-blonde hair flowed over her shoulders, unimpeded by any of the mysterious trinkets women keep at the hair-binding ready. My attention drifted to her gigantic flat tooth. She squeezed her eyes shut and opened her mouth like she was screaming, but no sound came out.

Bosco broke the silence. "Is she okay?"

"I feel like poop," Katie said, and then again, "I just want..."

"We need beer," I said. It had become imperative.

"You know, there's a bar right there," Bosco offered.

"Yes."

"Let's go in."

"It's too depressing to go in," Katie said, and she was right about that.

"Come on," said Bosco, "you can't just sit out here moaning. I'll talk them into giving us a pitcher."

I laughed at this, but it would be worth it just to see Bosco get shot down. He hopped up and opened the great oak door.

"I'll get us a pitcher," Bosco said. "I know I can get us a pitcher."

We wandered inside and filled up a booth. "Go get 'em," I said, slapping Bosco on the back.

Emboldened he slid up to the bar and approached the curly-haired bartender. From where we were sitting the conversation was lost, but as best I could tell Bosco said a whole lot of words. Then Curley said a couple words and seemed to grow a little bit taller. Bosco said some more words and Curley stared at him like a monk staring at a waterfall. Bosco shifted his weight, grabbed a handful of red straws out of a pint glass, and slumped back to us.

"No luck?" I asked.

"Pricks."

"Don't even bother with the other guy."

Katie said, "At this point they won't give us free drinks for anything. At this point it's a fun game for them not to."

"So basically we're screwed."

"Should we go?" I asked.

"I'm too lazy," Katie sighed. "Let's just sit here."

A moment passed. One of those awkward moments where you know the next thing someone says is destined to be either stupid or significant, and you don't really want to risk being the one who says it.

"You know," Bosco said, "we could take him."

This almost didn't register. "What?"

"He's big but if we ganged up we could take him."

"Take down the bartender, you're saying."

Another silence. This one not so awkward, more stunned. We were stunned. I saw stars sparkling off Bosco's lascivious grin.

"There's two of them," Katie reminded Bosco, who needed no reminding.

"Right, but there's what..." Bosco leaned out of the booth and started counting the room. "Ten other people in the bar. Altogether we could totally take these guys."

"Yeah, okay, and if we had a standing army we could take them, too."

"That's what I'm saying."

"Do you think they'll give me a glass of water?" Katie said.

"They have to give you water if you ask for it."

"No they don't."

Bosco slammed his fist on the burnt mahogany. "You have to give someone water. It's the humane thing to do."

"We aren't paying customers. We're lucky to be sitting here."

"Anyone can sit in a bar," Bosco insisted, "Anytime."

"That curly-haired guy keeps glaring at us," said Katie.

"So what?"

"So he might give me some water but he won't like it."

"Then let's take him down."

"You're crazy," I said.

Bosco poked a skinny red straw at my chest. "Why do you think bartenders pick up rounds from time to time? Why do you think there's such a thing as happy hour? Because there's more of us than there are of them."

We stared at Bosco with the gaze of two glass eyes looking up at their blind master for the first time.

"I'm just saying we could take them," Bosco shrugged, leaning back. "All of us together."

"Why would anyone else in this bar want to do that? Look at them. They all have drinks. They're all perfectly content."

"They all have overpriced drinks. Besides, it's Tuesday."

"Let's do it," Katie said all of a sudden.

All of a sudden—such a strange phrase. As if you could separate "a sudden" into parts. A sudden is instantaneous. There's no way you could suddenly do anything in any smaller quantity than all of it.

Anyway, all of a sudden Katie said, "Let's do it," and Bosco laughed at this, seeing how serious she looked, but she was even more serious than that. Really, I think she just needed some water, but she wanted a beer and so did I. And so did Bosco, I think. Though he may have just wanted to start some shit.

"All we have to do is talk three people into it," Katie explained. "That'll make six of us vs. two bartenders, with seven other customers of uncertain loyalties. Of those seven, even assuming none of them come around and join-in, we can count on the majority not interfering in any way. That's three who might take the side of the bartenders, but even so we'd still outnumber them."

It was as if she'd planned it all out ahead of time, sitting outside quietly, back against the brick wall, putting everything together, just waiting for someone else to suggest it.

She went on: "Now, other customers might come in. So we need one guy watching the door. I'm not worried about the back. It's not like we're going to hold this place all night. If there are any heroes in the crowd, we should have the bartenders subdued by the time they try to get involved. And by then we'll outnumber them more than two to one. And that's IF three of them come against us. And that's a big if. We're in a bar. We're in the Ritz. It's Tuesday afternoon. And we can offer discounts."

"You're saying we start selling?"

"We have to continue to maintain the business during the period of insurgency. We owe them that much. Besides, if we don't, any patrons acting as neutral parties would quickly turn against us. So it'll be discounts—not free drinks. If you want to drink free, you better have been involved in the raid."

"Do we have to call it a raid?" Bosco said.

"What else do you want to call it?"

"I want to call it a hijacking."

"That word is loaded," I said. "Let's call it a revolution."

"It's a raid," Katie said. "That's what we're calling it. No discussion."

"You aren't serious about this."

"Goddammit, Josh," Katie said. "I want a beer."

That was it. The fourth time she'd said it. There was

no going back now.

My job was to feel out the crowd. See who would be most likely to join up. We had to make sure we had our army before too many people knew what was going on. Word could get back to the bartenders, or worse, out onto the street, and then we'd be SOL, or DOA, or MIA, or any number of horrifying acronyms.

Katie went up to see if they would give her some water. She told us she was going to give them one more chance to be reasonable. Besides, this wasn't something she could do on a dry throat.

Meanwhile, Bosco was to case the joint. He was adamant we use the phrase "case the joint", and since he'd been shot down about "hijacking", Katie let him have it. Bosco checked the windows, scoped out the bathrooms, and made sure the back room was locked.

Things were looking up. Of the ten other customers clustered into three separate social groups, five seemed likely candidates. First, two gutter-punk kids drinking PBRs at the back table. Their names were Lilly and Marcus, a decent sort of folk, wearing a mixture of army green, goth black, and rainbow bright. They listened with amusement to our notion. But there was no amusement in Katie's voice. Not anymore. She'd been given her glass of water, but something had happened in the exchange that I will never understand. Maybe there'd been a severe intensity of rudeness in the bartender's obligation to give Katie the water. Maybe some words were exchanged. Fightin' words. Whatever it was, if the girl wasn't serious before, she was now.

Lilly and Marcus signed on eagerly. Both were scrawny, but I had no doubt they could scrap like the dickens in a surprise attack. We left them and their PBR and told them not to look suspicious and we'd signal them when it was time. Lilly volunteered to be our sentry, confident that she was the fastest among us. She had some rope in her bag that she admitted with a grin was used for Shibari, and offered it to the cause. We were gonna need it.

The booth full of anarchists gave us the surprising cold shoulder. At least they didn't give a fuck what we did, they just didn't want to be involved. We'd get no interference from them.

We still needed one more soldier.

When I sat down beside the young preppy-types in their Griz paraphernalia and Abercrombie glasses I felt like we may as well give up and go home. I said, "You guys haven't ever wanted to take over a bar by any chance, have you?" The younger of the three, a pretty-boy named James, probably thought I was looking for a way to hit on the girl he was with, and focused on contorting his face into the most apish scowl that ever chased-off a hippie. But the older kid, slightly overweight and three years away from a good balding, gave me a grin and asked if he would get college credit. The girl laughed at this, which was akin to receiving a thumbs-up from the Emperor of Rome. Her name was Molly and his was Ben, and they said to just tell them what to do.

Now we were seven. Eight if you count James, who I wouldn't rely on, but I knew he wouldn't turn on his buddies, so seven and a half let's say. Seven and a half enlisted, three conscientious anarchist objectors and an older couple sitting at the bar. When the shit went down Lilly would flash a charming smile and make sure this couple stayed put. We decided Curley had to go down hard. He was the muscle and the attitude. The only worry we had with Blondie was that he might pick up the phone or run out of the bar screaming. So the plan was this. Bosco, Katie, and I would ambush Curley, while Marcus and Ben contained Blondie. Once we had them down, Lilly would abandon her post and put her rope to use. It was this moment, when our sentry was down, that would be the most dangerous. If anyone came in then, the tables could turn on us.

The defining kick-off to the campaign was Ben's plan to get Blondie out of the picture.

"Gimme another," he said to Blondie, swaggering up with an empty glass. "Oh, and there's two people having sex in the bathroom."

As unlikely as this might have been on a Tuesday afternoon, Blondie was obligated to check it out. The Ritz' bathrooms were tiny. All he had to do was stick his head in and he'd see Ben was lying. That's why we put Molly in there. You may find it sexist, but we could never have pulled this off without her award-winning tits. Ben promised them a promotion to Sergeant Major, and by God they earned their stripes. As soon as she suckered Blondie inside, Ben followed behind to persuade him not to try and leave. At this point there could have been a fight, but we got lucky. Blondie just sat on the bathroom floor sulking for the next hour. I heard later that he and Molly got to talking and he didn't have such a bad time after all.

With Blondie out of the way, the wheels were in motion and we had no choice but to strike. It would only be a matter of time before Curley got suspicious. Bosco and Marcus snuck around behind the bar on hands and knees, much like a pair of drunken ninjas looking for a place to puke. Katie confronted Curley directly. There was some strange energy between them, something primal and aggressive. I flanked them, ready to leap across the bar and cut off access to the phone.

"I need more water," spat Katie, slamming down her empty pint glass. Curley looked at her long and slow. He took two steps in her direction.

"Why don't you go across the street? You can't just sit here and drink water all day."

"Yes I can. Anyone can sit in a bar. Anytime. For any reason. Give me some water."

"There's a sink in the bathroom. Go get it yourself."

Oh boy Curley was proud of himself for that one. He wore his smirk like a bow tie. Glaring at me as I leaned over the bar dangling on my elbows with a five-year-old grin, he snapped, "What do you want?"

"Beeeer!" I yowlped. This was the signal, and it all came down at once. Katie gave her pint glass a shove, launching it over the bar to shatter at Curley's feet. I've always felt this move was risky. Who wants to go into a battlefield covered in broken glass? But the gamble paid off. Curley jumped away from the glass and right into the ambush. Bosco hit him first, flying around the corner and tackling him at the knees. He hit him hard, too, managing to shove him backward into the menagerie of liquor. "Don't spill the whiskey!" someone cried. Then Marcus hit him from the other side. The bartender let out a strange guttural gurgle that sounded like a gopher trying to swallow a potato. Katie grabbed the well-spout and started blasting soda into the fray. I knew they'd be on the ground in seconds and I jumped the bar to join in. Curley was big and even with all three of us we had trouble keeping him down. Bosco took a clumsy hook to the jaw and reeled. I looked over and saw blood flowing freely from his nose. Katie let loose a mighty battle-cry, kind of a blah blah blah to the gods, and though we told her to take it easy she was overcome by the moment, and ran around the bar to pummel Curley with fists of doom.

"Stop it! What are you doing," Curley moaned. That's right, freak, cry about it. No one had really cut loose until then. Even with us infringing on sacred behind-the-bar territory, Curley hadn't given us all he could have, and we were more interested in restraining the boy so he could be tied up than assaulting him. If this came to court we didn't want to have to cough up anything for hospital bills. But Katie? Katie got her licks in.

At the end of it all, the three of us lay breathless against the back of the bar. Curley bound immobile in ropes and resigned to his fate. Bosco gave him a lazy slap on the knee. "That was goddamned invigorating!"

"Now what?" everyone asked.

Now the beer flows like wine and the wine flows like beer.

Halfway through my third pint, Ben and Molly came out of the bathroom holding hands. Ben turned down the gallant offer of our freshly invented whisquilameister special, and pulled me aside. "The other one, Blondie, he was hoping maybe we could tie him up too? He doesn't want anyone thinking he didn't put up a fight."

Understandable. I gave Ben some extra rope and told him he could even slap a shiner on the kid if he wanted, so long as Blondie was game.

Katie only served up one beer for herself. She drank it in silence, staring out across the blissful mayhem of our revolution. I sent Marcus and Lilly out to scrounge up bums and street-kids from off the main drag. To these we offered a full discount, RobinHood style. Half-price for everyone else. True to her word, Katie made the anarchists pay up in full.

By the time we slipped away, the place was hopping. There's nothing like cheap beer to light up a Tuesday night. And once the story began to spread, it spread fast. Who wouldn't want to say they bought a drink the day the Ritz got raided?

"I think we made more money for this place in the last hour than they make over the entire course of a regular Tuesday night," Katie said.

Ben thanked us for the good times. He told us he used to date Curley's sister and was pretty sure he could guarantee the whole thing to blow over. Still, he reckoned we'd better go before any cops show up.

The sun was going down. Katie and I headed across Higgins Street Bridge. Our beer circuits had been satisfied, but we were still dead broke. That's when someone who shall remain nameless said, "I want cheese fries."

He's in there somewhere.

Photo by BRAD WILSON

Made in the USA
Lexington, KY
20 April 2012